Arthur Edward Knox

Autumns on the Spey

With four illustrations by Wolf

Arthur Edward Knox

Autumns on the Spey
With four illustrations by Wolf

ISBN/EAN: 9783337374259

Printed in Europe, USA, Canada, Australia, Japan

Cover: Foto ©Andreas Hilbeck / pixelio.de

More available books at **www.hansebooks.com**

AUTUMNS ON THE SPEY.

BY

A. E. KNOX, M.A., F.L.S.

AUTHOR OF "ORNITHOLOGICAL RAMBLES IN SUSSEX," "GAME BIRDS AND
WILD-FOWL, THEIR FRIENDS AND THEIR FOES," ETC. ETC.

WITH FOUR ILLUSTRATIONS BY WOLF.

LONDON:
JOHN VAN VOORST, PATERNOSTER ROW.
MDCCCLXXII.

TO

CHARLES GORDON-LENNOX,

6TH DUKE OF RICHMOND, K.G.,

ETC. ETC.

THE FOLLOWING PAGES ARE GRATEFULLY

Inscribed.

PREFACE.

—◆—

THE greater part of this little volume is derived from letters written, on the spur of the
moment, to friends in the South, during
several autumns passed by the author at
Gordon Castle. He ventures to hope that
some of its pages may possess an interest
for the field naturalist as well as for the
salmon-fisher.

CONTENTS.

AUTUMNS ON THE SPEY.

A BIRD'S-EYE VIEW OF THE RIVER.

"The river nobly foams and flows,,
The charm of this enchanted ground,
And all its thousand turns disclose
Some fresher beauty varying round :
The haughtiest breast its wish might bound
Through life to dwell delighted here ;
Nor could on earth a spot be found
To nature and to me so dear."

BYRON.

ALTHOUGH most of the scenes and incidents described in the following papers have reference to that portion of the Spey which includes the last twelve miles of its rapid passage to the ocean, yet perhaps a rough sketch of its entire career, from its Highland cradle to its final disappearance in the North Sea—a distance of about a hundred miles—may not be unacceptable to the reader.

The Spey, then, rises in a small loch, more than 1200 feet above the level of the ocean, in the

B

district of Lochaber, among lofty precipitous mountains. This insignificant sheet of water, little more than a quarter of a mile in length, and considerably less in breadth, is the undoubted source of this glorious river; and although several tributaries fall into the parent stream, yet none are sufficiently important to deserve a higher title. During its early career, the surrounding hills are bleak, barren, and comparatively uninteresting, but where the new Highland railway crosses it, a few miles before reaching Kingussie, they assume a different character; and the traveller, while sitting at his ease in a coupé of the Limited Mail train, may enjoy for many miles one of the finest panoramic views of romantic scenery that the British Islands can afford. On the northwest the long chain of the Monadliadh—or grey —mountains stretches away into the distance. On the south-east rise the still loftier and grander Grampians, with Ben McDhui and Cairngorm, and other giants of the group, capped occasionally, even at this season, with snow. Gradually the hills on either side diminish, as they approach the river, until they terminate in an extensive valley advancing towards the north, through which the Spey meanders for many miles in the midst of most magnificent scenery. Several small lakes occasionally stud the face of the landscape, with, here and there, an old ruin perched on an island; the lesser hills that rise from their banks being clothed with evergreen fir-woods, while deep glens, covered with heather and surmounted by rocky peaks, fringed with birch-trees, succeed each other in endless variety, as the train rushes along. On reaching Kinrara, all these elements of the picturesque are seen to perfection. The rocks become wilder, and as if thrown about in confusion by a Titan's hand, and the birch woods denser and more extensive; but every now and then, open prairie-like glades, dotted with clumps of timber trees, appear as if by magic, and give a dash of civilization to the scenery. Beyond this the Spey may still be seen, winding between its rocky banks, and farther off the woods of Rothiemurchus clothing the hills in the middle of the picture, which, as the view recedes, become higher and higher, until the eye rests at last on the dark belts of perennially green pine forests, and beyond these again the irregular outline of the Grampians encloses the distant landscape.

After passing Grantown, the railway, which has hitherto nearly adhered to the direction of the old Highland road, finally deserts the neighbourhood of the river and pursues a north-western course, while that of the latter is about north-north-east. It thus flows through the celebrated Strathspey, passing Cromdale—which signifies crooked plain, from the semicircular sweep that the Spey takes close by the church and manse.* For several miles the hills forming the banks of the river are clothed with forests of pine, larch, and oak : its elevation here is about 600 feet above the sea.

A great variety of scenery follows for many miles. Well-wooded hills, cultivated farms, sandy plains, and barren heaths, succeed each other. Soon afterwards the Aven, the most important tributary of the Spey, falls in on the eastern side. The latter now progresses for many miles amidst picturesque scenery in the immediate neighbourhood of its course, passing near Ballindalloch, Carron, Wester Elchies, and Aberlour.

At Craigellachie the road runs close to the river, at the base of a precipitous bank clothed with fir-trees, which, in some portions of the rock, seem to have fixed their roots in the deep fissures of the granite. Between this and Arndilly, on the eastern bank, the Fiddich pours its tributary waters into the Spey, and the lofty hill of Ben Aigen appears, and forms the background of the picture

* DR. LONGMUIR's *Speyside.*

for many miles. Here the river turns to the left, and after making a semicircular sweep through the plain of Rothes, approaches "the pass of Surdon," but apparently is compelled by this promontory, which is only 237 feet from the opposite hill, to change its direction more to the north, which it pursues with little deviation during the remainder of its course.

Soon afterwards the Spey reaches "Boat o' Brig," where, as the name implies, there was formerly a ferry-boat; but the water is now spanned, not only by the viaduct of the Aberdeen and Inverness Railway, 245 feet in length, but by a suspension bridge, a little higher up. This bridge was erected after the memorable floods of 1829, which committed such terrible devastation in this part of Scotland, as to realize one's notions of almost the worst part of the Noachian deluge.

I have now attempted a hasty sketch of the progress of the river, from its origin in the little mountain tarn in Lochaber to Boat o' Brig. The distance from this to "The Tugnet," near Garmouth, where it discharges itself into the sea, is between ten and twelve miles.

Hitherto the course of the Spey has been through the heart of the Highlands, among strata of primæval structure, showing the result of central upheaval, in the highest degree, among the craggy mountains of the Grampians, whose peaks and precipices are composed of granite, gneiss, schist, quartz-rock, porphyry, and other crystalline masses, associated with limestone and micaceous slates. The very plains and valleys are the result of extreme denudation, and impress one with the conviction that the whole of this district was once under the sea. Even the old red sandstone seems to have been washed away, leaving the Silurian system, with its gneissose rocks, flagstones, and clays on the surface, or only covered by the comparatively recent glacial drift, or " till," which indeed prevails throughout all this part of Scotland. On reaching that portion of the river where I commenced this digression, we seem first to touch the inner edge of the long belt of old red sandstone that bounds the whole of the Moray Firth, from near the mouth of the Spey in a south-western direction, advancing up the Caledonian Canal nearly twenty miles further than Inverness, and from that town again towards the north-east, along the coast of Ross-shire, including Cromarty and Dornoch firths, and almost the whole of Caithness, where the belt attains its greatest width.

The ferruginous character of the rocks, and of

the dry burns on the right bank of that part of the Spey where we have now arrived, attest the presence of the old red sandstone. Geologists tell us that although the hills of this formation are less bold and precipitous than those in primitive districts, yet that they present great diversity of scenery, " here rising in rounded heights, there sinking in easy undulations, now swelling in sunny slopes, and anon retiring in winding glens, or rounded valley-basins of great beauty and fertility." The accuracy of this description is fully corroborated by the character and general aspect of the country through which the river here pursues its course. For some miles the right bank is bounded by a succession of pine-covered hills that stretch far away into the interior, occasionally presenting a steep declivity, supporting on its side numerous quaint-looking pinnacles of conglomerate, that seem almost ready to topple over and fall into many a dark pool below, where the rod-fisher can with difficulty obtain a footing on the narrow ledge, and must be master of "the Spey throw" to ensure successful sport—there clothed down to the very edge of the shingle with larch and spruce firs, in a gradual slope, and, still further on, showing the deep gorge of a now dry burn of considerable width, extending far back into the evergreen woods, and mounting higher and higher in such numerous and eccentric ramifications, that the eye would occasionally fail to detect their course, but for the zig-zag red lines that peep out every now and then, and the remarkable arenaceous cones of the same colour, which contrast beautifully with the dark verdure of the forest.*

This may give you a faint idea of the scenery at the mouth of the gorge known as "Alt Derg," or the red burn, about three miles above Gordon Castle, on the right bank of the Spey, immediately opposite to what used to be one of the best salmon pools in the river, but although those which occur "above bridge"† are not subject to such complete annual metamorphosis or total destruction, as affect almost all the others below it—and through the whole extent of three or four miles which may be said to comprise the *delta* of the Spey—yet such is the tremendous power of the winter floods, that the depth of the water and the character of the stream is liable to constant change, even here; pools being occasionally filled up with shingle, rocks, gravel, and débris of all kinds, and a considerable extent of the meadows and cultivated

* Readers who take an interest in the scenery of Scotland, viewed in connection with its physical geology, should consult the charming volume of Professor Archibald Geikie on this subject.

† The great bridge crossing the Spey near Fochabers.

fields on the left bank carried away, in spite of the persevering efforts of the landed proprietors to neutralize the effects of the flood, or to repair the damage by buttresses of timber enclosing huge masses of closely packed boulders, chevaux-de-frise of fir-trees, and similar contrivances to resist the torrent.

I have just said that the salmon pools between "Boat o' Brig" and the Spey bridge—which spans the river near Fochabers—preserve, less or more, their locality from year to year, although their depth and character are frequently altered; but the case is very different "below bridge." There are occasional exceptions to this—but they only serve to prove the rule. A more particular description of some of these pools may be attempted hereafter. This is only a rough sketch —a bird's-eye view, as it were, of the river and its shores.

For some miles past, the hills on the left bank have retired from the bed of the stream, and the rich alluvial plain is the site of several of the most fertile and highly cultivated farms in the north of Scotland. On nearing the bridge the higher ground gradually approaches the river, which here cuts its way for some distance through a rock of red sandstone; but shortly after, the cliff, gradually lowering, retires on the left, while on the right the pine-covered hills recede still further from the stream ; and now the well-timbered grounds of Gordon Castle open on the view, rising from the intervening plain, until the verdure of the deer-park, varied with heathery moorland, is succeeded by glens of deciduous trees and giant larches, beyond which a wide forest of primæval pines stretches for many miles over the hills, and forms a dark background to the picture, from which the old central tower of the Castle and the spire of Fochabers Kirk stand out in sharp relief.

Still lower down, the gorse-covered wastes and alder woods that flank the low shores, are regularly inundated by the winter floods, which, on retiring, leave numerous clear pools of water. Many of these, shaded from the sun, and protected from the drying winds of spring and summer, are never exhausted during the rest of the year, and become a favourite haunt of wild ducks and other water-birds during the later autumnal months.

I should have mentioned before this that the fall of the river between the bridge and the sea, a distance of nearly five miles, is considerable ; and as no cascade occurs in the interval, the force of the current throughout is necessarily very great.* Numerous rapids, as well as deep pools, continually succeed each other, and the water, even within a hundred yards of the sea, is perfectly fresh at all periods of the tide ; while from the frequent shifting of the bed of the stream, this river, although it ranks as the second in Scotland in its volume, draining not less than 1300 square miles of country, is not navigable.   Indeed to the realization of such an idea, fresh obstacles, more welcome to the salmon-fisher and the wild-fowl shooter than to the political economist, continually occur during this portion of its final course.

And now the "haughs," or real winter banks, of the Spey, withdraw gradually on either side ; the intervening space, sometimes more than a mile in width, being, in fact, the *delta* of the river ; a veritable wilderness of boulders and shingle, varied with islands and peninsulas, some mere sandbanks, others covered with alders, gorse, and bushes, through all of which it meanders in a perfect labyrinth of streams.   These occasionally meet, only to separate again ; and although they

* "It is the most rapid river in Scotland. Its fall for the last three miles of its course is sixty feet."—*Survey of the Province of Moray*, published at Aberdeen, A.D. 1798, page 98.

ultimately reunite just before reaching the sea, their tortuous course is sufficient to perplex even the experienced salmon-fisher, whose geographical recollections of the maze of last autumn are completely obliterated by the new vagaries in which the river has indulged during the " spates" of the previous winter.

A DISAPPOINTMENT.

---◆---

" Nonne vides
Regius ut placidâ tibi majestate per undas
Radit iter, liquidoque superbit gurgite Salmo.

. . . .
. . adversum quâ spumans ingruit amnis
Tollit ovans sese, et multo luctamine victor
Exilit."
JAMES PARKE (Lord Wensleydale),
Cambridge Tripos Verses, 1802.

IT was on a sunny afternoon in September that I started for a part of the river about two miles below Gordon Castle. "A southerly wind and a cloudy sky" are not such necessary conditions of success on the Spey as elsewhere, the rapidity of the stream generally ensuring sufficient disturbance on the surface of the water, although a dark day is always welcome to the fisherman.

The weather had been dry and sultry for a long time. There were but few heavy salmon in any, even of the best pools, and most of these had "tasted steel." The river was much lower than usual at this season, and the water transparently

clear, so that a single-gut casting line and a small
fly were indispensable. Day after day we had all
been longing for a fall in the barometer, to be
followed by a good " spate"* to bring up the large
fish from the sea, which were only waiting outside
for more water, to enable them to pass the bar,
rush up the stream, and reach their favourite pools.
The best season for the angler had but lately
commenced on this lower portion of the river.
The netting had ceased since the twenty-sixth of
August. Not a single kelt had yet been observed
on his or her downward voyage, and nothing was
wanting but a supply of fresh-run salmon, which
were now overdue.

From what I have said of the velocity of the
river, and the frequent and shallow rapids occur-
ring between the pools in this portion of its
course, you will be prepared to believe that the
fisherman must either throw his fly from the bank
or wade into the stream for that purpose, and
that a boat of any kind would be troublesome to
manage on its surface. Such, indeed, is the rule,
which in this instance, as in many others, may be
proved by a solitary exception. A small coble

---

* *Spate—spait—speat,* a flood.
Gaelic, *speid*—perhaps from *spe,* froth.—JAMIESON's *Dictionary
of the Scottish Language.*

can generally be seen, during the early morning, drawn up high and dry on the shingly beach near the bridge pool. This luxury, however, is reserved almost exclusively for the ladies, and as it draws very little water, can be navigated by the skilful boatman who always accompanies them— himself one of the best fishermen on the Spey— in perfect safety over all the rapids as far as the sea; but its return journey next morning is necessarily by road. A horse and cart, especially adapted for the purpose, meet it at the Tugnet, and convey it back to its usual station near the bridge. Sometimes a similar expedition takes place *up* the river, when "the overland route" being first accomplished, the fair anglers descend the stream from Boat o' Brig, passing the beautiful scenery on the right bank, which I have already described, and trying their fortune in the Couperee, the Chapel pool, the Rock pool, or the Greenbank, on the downward voyage, and seldom without considerable success.

You will conclude therefore, and truly, that, like my friend the heron, I am a wader; and indeed, without any desire to depreciate the advantages attending the use of a boat on certain rivers, or denying its absolute necessity on others, such as the Tay and the Tweed, yet every expe-

rienced salmon-fisher will coincide in my opinion
that in a rapid stream, with well-defined pools, it
is better to dispense with its services, and that an
indescribable charm is added to the sport by ab-
staining from any further aid than is afforded by
a perfect Macintosh equipment, and the attend-
ance of a clever clipper.

Apropos to this subject, I must tell you something of the individual who now accompanied me
in that capacity. My first experience of him was
at the commencement of the previous season.
He was then a little boy about twelve years of age,
and hardly strong enough, or tall enough, as I
fancied, to gaff a large salmon, or wade after me
into deep water, as would occasionally be necessary. But there was something very promising
about him. He was remarkably quiet and taci-
turn, and although at first a little awkward, yet,
before a month had elapsed, I found that, from
his natural intelligence, his love of the sport, and
his amphibious habits, he possessed, in embryo,
all the qualifications of a perfect aquatic gillie.
He soon became an adept with the clip, seldom
missing when he had a fair chance, and rarely
throwing one away; while to his coolness and
presence of mind in moments of difficulty, during
a long and exciting run, I have since frequently

been indebted for the successful capture of many
a heavy fish.

This was the beginning of Simon's second
season as my attendant, and as he had been down
this part of the river before, during the net-fishing
in the summer, I questioned him as to my pros-
pects of sport.

"Deed, sir, I canna say: I'm thinkin' there's
a wee bit too much sun the day."

"But how about the new pools? I see that the
river has not only struck out fresh channels for
herself since last year, but that, if I am not much
mistaken, the valley of boulders, that we are now
actually trudging over, must be the dry bed of
what used to be one of the best casts in the river,
where I killed the thirty-two pounder."

"Aye, is it, sir, the varra spot."

"But how many pools are there?"

"Well, I canna say—not many, that will hold
a muckle fish, until we get a good bit lower
down."

We had now walked over a considerable extent
of boulders and shingle, and reached the nearest
arm of the river, which appeared too shallow even
for a grilse, so wading though it, and again
traversing another peninsula like the last, and
crossing a second branch, which looked encourag-

C

ing, about a hundred yards lower down, I commenced operations there at once in a narrow but deep and turbulent pool, at the lower end of which I could just see the upper portion of a rapid, where the stream became wider and shallower, as it suddenly turned to the left and was then lost to view.

My first two throws were just above the boiling water through which the fly—a small black king —was whirled about in all directions. At the third, with a longer line, it dropped almost at the margin of the opposite bank, passed quickly through the whirlpool, and swam steadily through the strong current a few yards lower down. While my eye was fixed upon its movements, a sudden splash, close to the spot, gave the first promise of sport that had greeted me for many days. Only a rise it is true, but a real one. Half a dozen steps backwards, a few throws higher up, and the fly was over him. Another splash, but no hold of him yet. Once more I retired six paces, and now with increased excitement repeated the same process. A sudden plunge and a chuck told that I had got him this time.* First, he rushed up the stream, the line

* Notwithstanding the thrill of delight that electrifies every fisherman at the moment when he hooks a big salmon—especially

hissing through the water—then he sprang into
the air again and again, a splendid male fish—a
twenty-pounder at least, fresh from the sea, as
bright as silver, and with a distinct semicircular
seal-bite on his side, just underneath the dorsal
fin. This I noticed several times. Well, I
managed to keep above him, and played him up
and down the pool for nearly a quarter of an hour,
Simon in the meantime creeping cautiously
along the edge, gaff in hand, and eagerly watching for an opportunity to perform his part in the
ceremony. At last I tried to coax the fish within
his reach, but he was still too lively, and the water
too deep just under the bank, for the boy to clip
him there, so, after a few ineffectual attempts,
I turned his head down stream. This proceeding
would, of course, have soon reduced him to

---

if he has previously raised him unsuccessfully two or three times
—yet I never could share the feelings of some anglers of my
acquaintance who aver that they would *then* willingly hand over
the rod to a less fastidious sportsman, and that the subsequent
contest, and even the landing of your fish, are comparatively uninteresting. Such a proceeding appears to me to be precisely analogous to the conduct of a master of hounds, who, while hunting his
own pack, would, immediately after finding his first fox, call them
off in quest of a second, thus completely ignoring the pleasures of
the chase, the glorious excitement of the first burst, and all those
"moving accidents by flood and field" that constitute the great
charm of fox-hunting, and in which the true salmon-fisher equally
participates.

obedience if it could have been continued long enough, but we were now quickly approaching the lower rapid, and, as the force of the current gradually increased, the partially subdued fish resigned himself totally to its influence, the line ran out faster and faster, and my hope now was that by exercising as much gentle restraint as was possible under the circumstances, I might check his downward career sufficiently to enable Simon—who was already up to his knees in the middle of the shallow—to gaff him as he was passing. Down went the fish at a tremendous pace, floundering and wriggling over the stones like a gigantic eel, with his dorsal fin out of water. "Now, Simon, you have him!" I cried, as I saw the boy make a lunge with the clip; but the whizzing line told me too truly that the stroke had been unsuccessful, and the pace was too great to admit of its being repeated; so rushing along the bank and winding up whenever I had a chance, closely followed by Simon, I felt at that moment, as certain of ultimate success as a salmon-fisher *can* feel under any circumstances, for I knew that the hook, although a small one, must have a fair hold, and the single gut had already stood a severe test. The tail of the rapid was now within sight, and I anticipated no difficulty in bringing matters to a conclusion in the nearest pool below, when suddenly—just as my hopes were highest—I perceived, to my horror, another deep stream in front, running in from the left, and realized the unwelcome fact that I was on a peninsula, below and around which all was dark and turbulent from the meeting of the waters. What was to be done? The line was quickly running out. It was too late to retrace my steps, and though an expert swimmer under ordinary circumstances, I had previously experienced the danger of venturing out of one's depth in long, heavy, wading boots, such as I was wearing at that moment. My first impulse was to pull them off, and, rod in hand, to tread water down stream, landing on either bank, below the junction of the two arms of the river, but there was no time to carry out such an operation, even with Simon's assistance. The line was whizzing away, and a glance at the deep stream on the left—now rather above me, for I had waded out on the tongue of the promontory until the water had filled my boots and was up to my waist—revealed no hope in that direction. In agony I looked at the now emptying reel. But a few yards remained: these soon disappeared; the strain grew greater and greater: something *must* give way; the rod bent more and more, and then suddenly became —perfectly straight! I will not dwell on the misery of that moment. Frequently as they occur in the experience of a salmon-fisher, yet the bitterness of such mishaps never seems to be mitigated by repetition.

INCIDENT DURING A ROEDEER DRIVE.

———◆———

"Oft expectation fails, and most oft there
Where most it promises, and oft it hits
Where hope is coldest and despair most sits."
All's Well that Ends Well.

FOR some days afterwards, the weather continued
sultry and unfavourable for fishing. The blue
sky, unbroken by a single cloud, was as unpro-
mising as ever, and it was, therefore, with no
little pleasure I learned, one afternoon, that a
roedeer drive in the great fir-woods had been
arranged to take place on the following day.

It happened that my bedroom window commanded a view of a portion of these hills, and,
as I drew up the blind on that morning, the
scene, lovely as it always was, certainly seemed
to possess charms for me that I had never felt
before.

To the south, and immediately beneath me,
were the beautiful gardens and pleasure-grounds,
laid out in the Italian style, gorgeous with

flowers of every imaginable colour and variety, in the midst of which magnificent fountains threw their lofty jets of the clearest water high into air, or poured it, in mimic cascades, into wide basins below; while the lines of balustrade that separated this fairy land from the park on either side, were broken at intervals by urns of various sizes and forms, and statues of stags, or gigantic dogs, standing off in relief from the dense foliage of the lime-trees. Bounding the view in this direction, and contrasting powerfully with the Southern character of this home scene, rose the pine-covered hills, nearly two miles off, which wore to be the scene of our sport in a few hours; while a narrow cutting, exposing the tall stems, could be seen ascending from the base of the rising ground, like a clearing in an American forest. These fir-woods extended for miles far away towards the east, and round to the north-east, the "saw-edge" profile of their outline being backed by the sky, or, occasionally, by the heathery heights of more distant moorland.

When assembled at the appointed hour, we numbered about eight guns, and proceeded to the rendezvous on the outskirts of the wood. Here were already collected several keepers, clad in shooting dresses of Gordon tartan, and numerous

beaters to assist in driving. Operations commenced by our forming a line, about a quarter of
a mile long, the shooters being placed as nearly
as possible equidistant from each other; and thus,
with an extended front, we marched abreast
about a hundred yards up-hill, then wheeling to
the left, by word of command passed along from
the pivot flank, we drove the pine-forest diagonally, over great variety of ground, now up to
our knees in heather, and now descending the
steep and rugged slope of a dry red sandstone
watercourse, or scrambling up the opposite bank,
and endeavouring all the time to preserve our line
as nearly as possible—a difficult task while out of
sight of each other, or only catching an occasional glimpse of the nearest beater on either
side. Every now and then a distant shot, or two
or three in succession, would tell that a buck had
been killed, or was running the gauntlet, or
perhaps that a blackcock had been sprung by the
beaters. As yet I had seen nothing in the way
of game, except a few hares, and having no
intention of throwing away my ammunition on
them, my gun remained still undischarged—one
barrel loaded with buckshot, the other with No. 5
—and I was just beginning to grumble at my
bad luck, when we emerged all at once from the

tall pines, and came upon a wide extent of open moorland, studded with clumps and irregular patches of spruce and Scotch firs, of younger growth. Here an opportunity of "dressing up," in military parlance, was afforded to as many of us as were within sight of each other, although at least three-fourths of the field were out of view on either side. Finding myself considerably in the rear, I was running forward to the front, and had hardly plunged into one of the clumps that intervened, when a cry of "Roe! roe!" followed by a report from the right, reached my ears. Hurrying through the trees, I was just in time, as I emerged on the opposite side, to catch a glimpse of a fine buck, passing at full speed about thirty yards off. My first shot, directly in front of his shoulder, was unsuccessful; with the second he rolled over, and the next moment the hunting-knife of the nearest keeper finished his career; but I found that, notwithstanding my previous conviction of the impossibility of such a blunder, I had thoughtlessly discharged the barrel containing small shot first, which, at that distance, is rarely sufficient to bring a roedeer to the ground.

We were now among the haunts of the black game, and several noble male birds of that species

fell at intervals along the line, soon after which
we converged upon our centre, and a halt was
called. Some time elapsed, however, before all
the stragglers, shooters as well as beaters, were
collected together. Now and then, a keeper
might be seen, slowly crawling through the
heather, with a buck or a doe slung over his
shoulders, while another would appear from the
opposite quarter, with feathered game or hares
in either hand, until at last all were assembled,
and the varying fortunes of each sportsman
hurriedly related during the brief time allotted
for luncheon.

And now the " drive " was about to assume a
totally different character. As yet, we had been
unassisted by any dogs, except a few sedate re-
trievers, who walked listlessly behind their masters,
and preserved their grave demeanour, unless, when
occasionally put on the track of a wounded roe or
a winged blackcock, when their services proved
invaluable ; but now I first observed, in charge of
a new batch of keepers, a motley pack of dogs, of
various sizes and breeds, conspicuous among
which was a huge black and tan bloodhound, of the
true musical, long-eared type—a host in himself,
I was assured, and especially adapted to the kind
of sport that was now about to commence.

A short walk from this spot took us to a new portion of the forest, on more elevated ground, where, instead of the lofty primæval pines that clothe the base of the hills, we found ourselves among Scotch firs of lesser stature ; their trunks naked for some distance from the ground, above which their horizontal branches grew thickly in all directions. We were now walking along silently, in single file, when the keeper who was conducting us suddenly stopped, and pointing to a tree at a little distance, directed the shooter who was nearest to him to take up his position among its branches. An ordinary passer by would have seen nothing to attract his attention, but a more careful examination revealed a mass of boughs, like a huge bird's nest, about twelve or fourteen feet overhead, with a rude and frail ladder of fir-sticks fastened to the trunk, leading up to it almost perpendicularly, and suggesting altogether the idea of a so-called gorilla's dormitory, but seeming to evince less architectural talent in its construction than that quadrumane would have exhibited. These hiding-places were arranged in trees about a hundred yards apart from each other, and in due time I found myself concealed in the particular one allotted to me. Then I could per-ceive that the apparent rudeness of the details was intentional—a few bark-covered sticks, nailed together, formed the floor, the sides were equally simple, and through these the living boughs were roughly interwoven.

Some time elapsed before all the gunners were located in their respective trees, during which I had ample leisure to study my position. I found that it commanded a narrow vista, immediately in front, intersected by a path or favourite run of the roedeer. These tracks were well-known to the keepers, and the trees containing our nests were selected by them for the sake of any advantages of this kind that they seemed to possess. To the right and left the dense foliage shut out the view, but immediately behind me the ground was comparatively open, and several firs, taller than the one in which I was concealed, rose out of the heather, the upper branches of one of the nearest, loaded with cones, hanging almost over my head. Through an interval between these loftier trees, I perceived that I was on the ridge of a hill; for a little lower down, the summits of the pines alone were visible; and as the ground sloped away in that direction, I could catch a glimpse of the Spey, like a streak of bright silver, and still further off, the blue mountains of the distant Highlands.

I should have mentioned that, during the time occupied in placing us at our different stations, the hounds had been taken, by a circuitous route, through the woods to a considerable distance, accompanied by an army of beaters, and as soon as all was ready, the report of a single gun announced the fact to the huntsman, who, at once, with all his assistants, human and canine—the former drawn out in a line—commenced operations. The denseness and great extent of the pine-forest, and the undulating nature of the ground, for a long time prevented my hearing any sounds proceeding from that direction, but presently the distant report of a gun, quickly followed by another, told me that a roe was already on the move, and that some fortunate sportsman had not been long kept in suspense. The day, like so many that had preceded it of late, was close and sultry, and the persecution that I endured from gnats and midges far beyond anything of the kind I had previously experienced. Their attacks, indeed, as I found on many subsequent occasions, constitute the standard plague of a roedeer drive in these woods. When seated on the ground, the victim is most severely punished. The retreat among the boughs above furnished somewhat of a sanctuary, but even here it is bad enough. Smoking seems to afford a temporary relief, and to repel the enemy for a time, but no sooner is the pipe empty, or the cigar finished, than these Lilliputian tormentors recommence their attacks, and give even the un-travelled sportsman a fair idea of the powers of the musquito in India, or of the swarms of gnats in Norway and Lapland.

I had just finished my fourth pipe, when the distant sounds of dogs and men fell on my ears. The *chasse* was evidently approaching. A shot soon followed from the same quarter, the yells and shouts became louder, and the cry of the hounds more distinct. Pre-eminent above all was the deep baying of the bloodhound, who was appa-rently following a line of his own, and gradually, but perceptibly, nearing my position. Now it ceased altogether, then suddenly recommenced within a hundred yards of me. It was an excit-ing moment as I knelt down in the nest, and, with my finger on the trigger, fixed my eyes on the spot where the deer-path crossed the narrow vista in front of me. Presently the loud and con-tinuous notes of the bloodhound told that he was close on his quarry, and I felt sure that he was driving it towards me ; then followed a rush and a crackling of the rotten sticks, close by, but

instead of a goodly buck, as I had fondly expected, out bounded a poor little fawn, and stopped
for a few seconds in the opening, trembling and
looking about, as if not knowing in what direction
to fly from its persecutor. There it stood, within
twelve yards of me, an easy victim, but I could
not find it in my heart to pull the trigger. On it
passed, the hound soon crossing at the same spot,
and pertinaciously sticking to the scent, although
no match in pace for the animal he was pursuing.
Long and anxiously did I listen, until his deep
notes gradually died away in the distance, and
as no shot was fired afterwards in that direction,
I concluded that the poor thing had run the
gauntlet in safety, and congratulated myself sincerely on having abstained from thoughtlessly
putting an end to its existence.

For full an hour afterwards did I keep watch,
staring at the opposite path, at first anxiously,
then listlessly, in the vain hope of seeing a buck
pass, although roused every now and then as the
shouts of the drivers occasionally reached my
ears, or the tonguing of a hound, gradually approaching but finally passing unseen, like the
animal he was chasing, raised my expectations to
the utmost for a few moments. At last, becoming
resigned to my bad luck, I turned round in my

place of concealment and again admired the
glimpse of the distant landscape between the taller
trees in the opposite direction. Nothing had
struck me more throughout the day than the perfect stillness of nature, the uninterrupted silence
reigning in these fir-woods. With the exception
of the solitary fawn, I had neither seen nor heard
any native animal since I ascended to my place
of concealment. I was especially surprised at
the total absence of all kinds of small birds,
some of which, such as the great tit, the blue tit,
or their congeners, the marsh or the cole tit, I
should have expected to see or hear even at this
season, or at least to have caught a glimpse of
some feathered inhabitants of the forest. This
circumstance had just recurred to my memory
with redoubled force, as I perceived, by the de-
clining sun, that the evening was approaching,
when suddenly a singular, continuous, shrill
chirping sound reached my ears, as of several
small birds together, but the notes were strange
to me. Although well acquainted with the call
of most British birds, I could not recognize this
one, and the longer I listened the more I was
puzzled. Gradually it approached, and seemed to
proceed from one of the taller Scotch firs at a
little distance. Fixing my eyes on the spot, I

soon saw several little birds, something larger than
bullfinches, emerging from the foliage, and, flying
one by one towards the tree that was nearest to
me, alight on the very boughs that hung over my
head.   I could hardly believe my eyes, as I realized the delightful fact that I was actually within
a few yards of a whole family of crossbills, *loxia
curvirostra*, busily engaged at their marvellous
employment of splitting the fir-cones and extracting the seeds.

Need I say that the recollection of previous
bad luck, and even my sufferings from the gnats,
were obliterated by such an interesting sight, not
the less welcome from its being so unexpected.
The very plumage of these little creatures added
to the charm of their presence.   Some were of a
beautiful deep crimson colour, others orange or
yellow ; others, again, were clad in a plain brown
livery, and all were busily intent on their occupation
of rifling the cones, during which they kept flying
about from one twig to another, incessantly uttering their shrill, monotonous notes.   After close
observation, I noticed that they seldom attempted
to operate upon a cone on the exact spot where it
grew, but after snapping one off from a slender
terminal twig, each bird would hop or fly to the
central part of the branch, and in parrot-like

fashion hold it in his foot, but more frequently *under* it, as a hawk holds a small bird when in the act of devouring it, and quickly inserting his bill between the scales, split them open by means of that wonderful tool, and extract the seeds with the greatest facility. Occasionally a cone would fall to the ground just as it was snapped off; but, in such a case, a fresh one was instantly selected, no further notice being taken of the one that had dropped. Their powers of climbing appeared fully equal to that of the titmice, as they swung about in all directions and in every imaginable attitude, twisting and twirling, fluttering and chattering, within a few yards of me, and evidently quite unconscious of my presence. This was too good to last. The loud cries of the beaters, now rapidly approaching, had for some time overpowered the notes of the crossbills, and announced that the *chasse* was drawing to a close. Either alarmed at this, or having completed their selection of the most tempting cones in the fir-tree over my head, some of the little birds were evidently preparing for a move, when suddenly a rushing sound behind me recalled me to consciousness, and turning about, I had just time to catch a glimpse of a fine roebuck, with a capital head, dash across the vista within twelve yards of my position. My gun, on half-cock, had long reposed in the hollow of my arm, and there it still remained, as useless, under the circumstances, as a walking-stick. I will not venture to assert that I felt no mortification at that moment, nor when relating the incident to some of my more successful brother sportsmen afterwards, but I can sincerely say that the disappointment was more than compensated by the rich ornithological treat I had the good fortune to enjoy.

A FRIEND IN NEED.

—◆—

" He flies aloft and flounces round the pool,
  Indignant of the guile.   With yielding hand
  That feels him still, yet to his furious course
  Gives way, you, now retiring, following now
  Across the stream, exhaust his idle rage."
                                   THOMSON'S *Seasons*.

ABOUT a week had elapsed since my last visit
to the lower part of the river, when a sudden fall
in the barometer promised a change for the better.
This expectation was encouraged by the fact that
the wind had veered round to the north, the wet
point in this part of Scotland, where the German
Ocean performs the same duty as the Atlantic in
the western and south-western portions of the
island.   Our hopes of a spate, however, were disappointed. The rain, it is true, fell over the Moray
Firth and the adjacent districts, but seemed to
have exhausted its treasures before reaching the
Highlands to the south, where the lesser tributaries
of the Spey, of late nearly dried up, derive their
sources, and materially affect the state of the water.

Nevertheless, although perfectly transparent, it appeared to have risen a few inches, quite sufficient, under the circumstances, to encourage the hopes of an ardent salmon-fisher; and it was with a secret feeling of satisfaction that I now found myself "told off" to the very part of the river that had been the scene of my previous disappointment.

On this occasion I was accompanied by a young friend, whom I shall call A, and the boy Simon, who was to perform the duties of clipper for both of us; and, as we were likely to be employed in different pools during the day, we provided ourselves with shrill whistles, by the use of which we could summon him to our assistance as we might respectively require his services; the human voice being more easily drowned in the noise of the rapids.

I have already said that as the Spey approaches the sea, it, or "she"—as the river is always designated here—divides into several branches. Some of these, after running for half a mile or more, again join the main current. Thus—as I had now good reason to remember—one may find one's self occasionally on the point of a peninsula, with a stream roaring on both sides. If too deep to cross in wading boots, and with a big fish at the end of one's line rushing down, he is as good as lost. But I had now guarded against the probability of such an accident by substituting my long Macintosh overalls, reaching upwards as high as the chest, supported over the shoulders by short braces, and tightly fastened round the waist by a hempen* cord to prevent the ingress of water to the lower regions ; while thick, short, worsted socks, and large, well-nailed brogues, buckled over them, completed my equipment.

Frequently since last week had I thought over my late mishap, and mentally recapitulated every incident that had occurred, and as often derived consolation from the conviction, that, unless I could have crossed the upper part of the rapid, where Simon had failed in his attempt to clip the salmon, or over the stream that cut me off on the left, I could not have prevented the catastrophe. All this was passing through my mind for the hundredth time, as, after separating from *A*,— whom I left with Simon at a pool on the right bank of the main current,—I waded over to the opposite side, a little above the scene of my former

* I have found this better than a leather strap, as it tightens when wet, whereas the latter becomes relaxed if saturated with water.

adventure, impelled by an uncontrollable desire to
try the same spot again. Not that much had as
yet occurred to excite my hopes. We had agreed
to use different flies, and neither my companion
nor I had as yet raised a single salmon, although
we had tried several kinds in succession, and in
likely places. I was just beginning to think that
the river had not risen sufficiently to bring up any
fresh fish from the sea, or even to induce the few
she already contained to change their quarters,
when I found myself close to the top of a rapid,
and immediately below it a boiling pool, which I
at once recognized as the identical place where I
had hooked my runaway last week, and as I looked
at the spot I could not help feeling the disappointment keenly renewed. The sun was now
low in the horizon, and putting on a brighter fly,
but with little hope of a rise—indeed almost
mechanically—I threw into the torrent, and when
the line was straight worked it out into the deep
water at the side. Splash! A rise, but fortunately no touch on the hook. How my heart
beat! for I knew by the vigour of the plunge that
it was a large salmon. However, I did not forget
to repeat the prudent tactics of an old fisherman
on this occasion, and walking back six paces, I
slowly retraced them as before, with a throw at

each step—taking especial care to preserve the same length of line. Just as I took the sixth and last, and as the fly touched the water, another plunge, and a simultaneous turn of the wrist on my part was followed by a chuck; then fiz—fiz— and away went the fish down stream, making straight for the dreadful rapid below. Suddenly he turned right about face, and I had hardly time to wind up the slack line when he sprang high out of the water, revealing to my astonished sight the identical hero of my former adventure. There was no mistaking him. Short and thick, in proportion to his length, with his blue back and silvery sides, and the same crescent-shaped seal-bite just below the dorsal fin. But the odds were all against his speedy capture. I whistled, and whistled, and even shouted, in vain, to attract the attention of Simon or of A. The roar of the torrent drowned every other sound. At last the boy caught a glimpse of my rod, bent like a bow, and as I threw a hurried glance up the river, I saw my friend, who had been trying the pool just above, fling down his own rod, and snatching the gaff from the reluctant Simon, run to my assistance at his best speed, but still at the opposite side of the stream, and lower down than where I had crossed. Here he at once commenced wading, but the passage was necessarily a tedious task, the increased force of the current at this spot rendering great care necessary, while the splendid fish, all this time, kept rushing about and leaping high out of the water, evidently, as I believe, trying to fall on the casting-line momentarily rendered slack by his somersaults, but fortunately he did not succeed in this manœuvre, and then taking to sulking, down he went to the bottom.

We had now time to hold a council of war, and we arranged that if the salmon should ultimately repeat his former tactics, I should try to coax him over the shallowest part of the rapid in his descent, while *A*, having taken up his position there beforehand in the water, would look out for his back fin and endeavour to gaff him as he passed—the very operation in which Simon had previously failed. In the event of this not succeeding, I made up my mind to wade across to the opposite side of the river, taking care to have as little line as possible out at the time : thus I should not be stopped by the deep stream lower down on the left, which had cut me off on the former occasion. However, the first step was to rouse the fish out of his sulky fit. Here great delicacy combined with firmness was of importance, for the water was exceedingly transparent, and, together with the brightness of the weather, and the shyness of salmon at present, necessitated the use of very small flies and single gut casting-lines. Anything, therefore, like violence in dealing with a large fish must have been followed by its instantaneous loss. The first point, then, was to compel him to move, while I kept up a steady and regular pressure on as short and perpendicular a line as possible. *A* therefore waded in and threw a large stone just above him; then a second, and a third. Away he went again, and as I succeeded in coaxing him at last into a little bay of dead water, I was in great hopes that we should have gaffed him there; but he got a sight of the clip, and darted off once more into the middle of the current: however, he was now too weak to work upwards, or even to resist its force, so turning his head down stream, he dashed resolutely at the rapid, repeating, as nearly as possible, his previous performance. This was the crisis. *A* got to the middle of the water, while I took a hasty survey of the place where I *must* wade or swim over if he missed the clip. All this occurred in a few seconds. Down went the fish over the shallows, his back fin and the upper part of his tail appearing above the surface; but the pace was tremendous, and I dared not attempt to check it by an increased pressure on the line. At this moment, just as he was approaching his fate, he rushed into a deeper part of the rapid, *A* resolutely plunging after him, and almost inserting the clip; but the force of the current, and the sudden exertion combined, carried my friend off his legs, and in an instant his long Macintosh stockings filled with water, and he was swept down some distance, but fortunately recovered his footing, and getting safely back to shore, prepared, if necessary, to swim over to my assistance after I had crossed. As for myself, the moment I saw that the fish had escaped, and was carried down the rapid towards the deep water, I waded over to the opposite side, according to our previous arrangement. It was just as much as I could do without swimming. The round boulders at the bottom, already pressed upon by the force of the stream, seemed to fly from under my feet, buoyed up as I was by the air confined in the legs of the overalls. As I got close to the land, the water was up to my armpits, and I had a struggle to climb the bank and to keep the rod upright all the time, while the line was whizzing away, and it seemed doubtful, for a few moments, whether the reel would not be emptied before I obtained a footing on *terra firma*,

and the misfortune of last week be repeated.
Once there, however, I felt almost sure of ultimate
success; and I saw *A*—who, by the way, is a
capital swimmer—plunging in from the opposite
shore, having got rid of his Macintosh stockings,
and coming to my assistance, and by the time he
was over I had run down stream and wound up at
least three-fourths of a hundred yards of line.
From this spot, almost as far as the sea, the river
pursues her tortuous course, more intricately than
ever, in a succession of rapids and small pools.
Here and there, near the upper part of the former,
it was easy to cross by wading, and once more
passing over to a long stretch of shingle, at the
other side, I managed to lead my fish, now nearly
tired out, down stream for a considerable distance,
without meeting any formidable obstacle. His
dying struggles during the latter part of the run
had evidently attracted the attention of a great
black-backed gull, who, accompanied by several
immature birds of the same species, continued to
soar over our heads, every now and then darting
down close to the salmon as he turned over helplessly, and his bright silvery sides gleamed through
the water; doubtless watching, with the true scavenger instinct, for the moment of dissolution,
though apparently unconscious of the cause of his

difficulties, and quite ignoring the presence of his persecutors. Now, at last, I was preparing to pilot him into a promising little haven of backwater lower down, which was soon reached, but the great force of the current carried him past, in spite of all my manœuvring. That was a critical moment. If the hold of the hook had been less firm, or the gut any but the very best, I must have lost him, for I suddenly saw, to my dismay, that we were again on the extremity of another promontory, a second wide stream running in a little below us, and the dark water showing everywhere the increasing depth of the river. Now or never! I put on a strong but steady pressure; gradually the half-exhausted fish yielded so far as to roll heavily towards the side. His back fin is at last visible, now his broad fan-like tail appears for a moment. In dashes *A*, and in the very nick of time, just as we arrive at the junction of the two currents, makes a bold stroke with the clip. Bravo! the prize is ours, and I am on the point of lowering the rod, when, to my horror, I see the gaff break off short in the hand of my friend. Our fate hangs on a hair. The next moment I lose sight of all except his head, but in an instant afterwards he reappears, clasping with both arms a goodly salmon—twenty-two pounds' weight—as

J. Wolf. del.

THE LAST CHANCE

M & N Hanhart lith.

Page 46.

it struggles vainly to escape from his fond but firm embrace. It was indeed " the last chance," and I could not help feeling that the successful termination of the adventure was due to the assistance of my friend, or, to say the least, that " the honours were divided ; " and I never more sincerely acknowledged the truth of the old familiar adage,

"A friend in need is a friend indeed."

FERÆ NATURÆ.

———◆———

"The numerous forests and schases are very profitable for feiding of bestial and delectable for hunting. They are full of reid deer and roes, woulffs, foxes, wyldcatts, brocks, skuyrells, whittrets, weasels, otters, martrixes, hares and fumarts."—SIR ROBERT GORDON's *History of the Earldom of Sutherland*, A.D. 1630.

ALTHOUGH nearly two hundred and fifty years have elapsed since the above passage was written, yet all the wild animals here enumerated—with the exception of the wolf *—are still to be met with in the North of Scotland, to the entire of which region we cannot doubt that these remarks were applicable, although a very perceptible local increase in certain species, and considerable diminution in others, have taken place during the last twenty or thirty years.

While investigating this subject a few years ago,

---

* "In Ireland, a species of wolf continued to exist until the year 1710. In Scotland, to the year 1680. In England, it was extirpated at a much earlier period."—OWEN's *British Fossil Mammals.*

in reference to the neighbourhood of Gordon
Castle, I was much surprised, and not less
interested, to find that the squirrel, *Sciurus vulgaris*, by no means rare and still gradually
increasing, had been totally unknown even to
young men in the days of their boyhood. In the
highlands of Banffshire, indeed, many shepherds
and foresters with whom I conversed had never
seen the animal at all, even in the wooded glens
and corries—a familiar description of its characteristic form, actions, and habits failing to enable
them to identify it—and on pursuing my inquiries
still further in the lower districts, where it is now
of common occurrence, I found the popular belief
universal that it was unknown in Morayshire and
Banffshire until a few years ago, when "the Pilgrim
Fathers" of the race were supposed to have crossed
the Caledonian Canal from Invernesshire, and that
even these, like the lords of the creation, were
descended from a single pair, which were introduced a few years before by a benevolent lady, who,
having frequently admired their lively habits and
sprightly attitudes during her visits to England,
created a Garden of Eden for them within the
sacred precincts of her park. Not long afterwards
I had the opportunity of becoming acquainted with
that accomplished naturalist, the Rev. Dr. Gordon

E

of Birnie, near Elgin, and learned from him that the prevalent faith in the above story was founded on fact, in corroboration of which, after renewing his inquiries, he has lately communicated to me the following particulars :—

"Squirrels, which now abound on both sides of the Moray Firth, were introduced into this district of Scotland in 1844, when Lady Lovat turned out a few at Beaufort Castle, west of Inverness. They appeared at Kilravock in 1851, at Cawdor in 1855, and had spread so far into Elginshire in 1860 as to have been observed at Birchfield in the glen of Rothes. They crossed the Spey a few years ago, and are now to be met with on the banks of the Doveran in Banffshire, while on the northern shores of the Moray Firth they made a like progress from the Beaufort woods, and were observed in 1858 at Kilmuir Castle.

"At Cawdor, Altyre, and elsewhere, they have multiplied to a great extent, and have become very injurious to the Scotch fir and larch, though chiefly to the former. They are fond of the cones, or rather the seeds, of the spruce fir, but have not been known to touch its bark as they do—most destructively—that of the Scotch fir and larch.

"It is certainly remarkable that these animals should have disappeared for so long from a district where there must always have been sufficient wood to shelter them, and where, of late years, they have been spreading so vigorously and extensively.

" In order to diminish their numbers, and thus in some measure save the plantations from their attacks, premiums have been offered. Mr. Stables, Lord Cawdor's agent, in kindly furnishing me with the following memorandum of the squirrels killed on the Cawdor property, tells me that it is only by shooting that their numbers can be reduced. A terrier dog is very useful, as it runs the scent to the tree they have gone up, and barks very keenly, giving notice to the man in search of them.

Note of the number of squirrels killed on the Cawdor plantations :—

" In 1862—469	" In 1867—1164
1863—617	1868—1095
1864—468	1869— 503
1865—609	1870— 867.
1866—779	

" Mr. Stables remarks that the number killed each year depended a good deal on the qualifications of the men employed, and on the price paid for each tail. He also relates the following anecdote :—

" ' Soon after the squirrels made their first

appearance in Nairnshire, I recollect crossing the hill between the glen of Holme and the Streens, on the Findhorn. While on the top of the bare hill, one of the men who were accompanying me, but a little distance from me at the time, was startled by his sheep-dog becoming very excited, and barking at "a queer wee beastie" among the heather. The beastie, to avoid its persecutor, and seeing no other place of refuge in that tree-less region, at once made for the man himself, and at one bound gained the crown of his bonnet, to the poor fellow's sad discomfiture, for he deemed himself assailed by something that was, at least, "uncannie."' Mr. Stables adds, 'The fact of a squirrel being thus found on a bare elevated moor, at least a couple of miles from the nearest wood or tree, shows that it was in the act of migration.'"

Later in the autumn of the same year in which I first heard this singular story of the reappearance of the squirrel in the North of Scotland, I was staying on a visit at The Hirsel in Berwickshire, near Coldstream, and on mention-ing it to Lord Home, he was much struck by the account, and assured me that the restoration of the same species to the South of Scotland had been brought about in a manner precisely similar, though at an earlier period. The coincidence is certainly remarkable. Squirrels were unknown there seventy years ago, but about that time his lordship's grandmother, Elizabeth, Duchess of Buccleuch, turned out a few at Dalkeith. Before long they increased rapidly, and several were observed at Arniston, twelve miles off. From thence they spread into Selkirkshire, but, from some cause not ascertained, their further progress seemed to be arrested for a time, until about 1841, when the first squirrel made its appearance at The Hirsel, to the great astonishment of the people in the neighbourhood, who had never seen one before. In this district, though now generally distributed, they are comparatively harmless, and escape persecution; their favourite food consisting of the nuts of hazel and beech which, with other deciduous trees, abound in the adjacent woods and along the banks of the Tweed; but Lord Home says that he has been obliged to reduce their numbers on his property at Douglas Castle, in Lanarkshire, where their depredations have caused serious injury to the plantations of larch and Scotch firs. Alas! it is in vain for even their best friends to pronounce a verdict of " not guilty." No one was ever more anxious than myself to credit and, if possible, prove their

innocence. Nothing short of ocular demonstration could have converted me ; and although I
have never succeeded in detecting any external
injury inflicted on either spruce or Scotch firs,
yet the testimony of Dr. Gordon and others
whom I have quoted must be allowed to overrule
my negative evidence, while I have been too often
an unwilling witness of the havoc they commit
among plantations of larch. The tender bark is
a favourite morsel, and exhibits unmistakable
excoriations from their teeth, and when the juicy
terminal shoot at the top of the tree has just
made its appearance, in the warm days of Spring,
it would, after all, be as reasonable to suppose
that a squirrel should resist such a temptation, as
to expect a similar act of self-denial on the part
of a London alderman when the young asparagus
first comes into season.

The disappearance of this hardy little quadruped for so many years previous to 1844, from a
district where—as Dr. Gordon has observed in
reference to Morayshire and Invernesshire—
" there must always have been a sufficient quantity of wood to shelter them," is certainly " remarkable," and, in the absence of any ostensible
cause, the field of conjecture is thrown open. In
the list of wild animals enumerated by the old

historian of Sutherland, which I have prefixed to this chapter, the martrix, or marten, *Martes foina*, is included. From its arboreal habits, as well as its carnivorous propensities, it appears to me that none would have been so likely to have acted as a check on the increase of the squirrel, and although the excessive preservation of game and consequent persecution of predatory animals, of late years, in the moors and forests, have greatly reduced the number of martens, even in their favourite retreats, and actually exterminated them in others where they were once of common occurrence, yet we know that they abounded in the Highlands during the first half of the present century. For example, on the Glengarry property alone, a friend of mine, when lessee, destroyed no less than 246 martens between 1837 and 1840. Now, it is just possible that the excessive prevalence of this species, and the scarcity of the squirrel, may have been contemporaneous— a supposition to which the rapid increase of the latter in Invernesshire during the last thirty years would appear to lend some colour.

The "whittret," or stoat, *Mustela erminea*, and the weasel, *Mustela vulgaris*, though less numerous than formerly, are still of ordinary occurrence, and figure conspicuously in "the gamekeeper's larder." The "fumart," or polecat, *Mustela putorius*, is rare, while the "brock," or badger, *Meles taxus*, and the wild cat,* *Felis catus*, have retreated to the comparatively inaccessible strongholds of the rocks and mountains. Indeed the latter animal has become exceedingly scarce. I never met with one in the wild state, and the only living example I have seen in Scotland was at Balmachan, confined in a large iron cage—a full-grown male, whose great size, powerful frame, and demoniacal expression fully entitled him to the appellation of a "British tiger."

The otter, *Lutra vulgaris*, still survives, though gradually yielding to persecution. I have long felt satisfied that the depredations of this beautiful and graceful quadruped are far less serious than is generally supposed. In the smaller streams and burns they certainly consume a number of trout, but, as a set-off to this, they

---

* The still popular belief that this species is the source of our domestic stock is incorrect. The anatomical distinctions are sufficiently obvious to settle the question. A German traveller, Dr. Rüppel, is believed by Temminck to have discovered a species of cat in Abyssinia from which at some remote period our useful mousers derived their origin, but our own accomplished zoologist, Bell, considers that "we have yet to seek for the true original of this useful, gentle, and elegant animal."

kill quantities of pike wherever that voracious
fish has contrived to establish itself. As to
salmon, they rarely capture one of considerable
size, while the arch-enemy of the species, the
seal, *Phoca vitulina*, has become quite a rare
visitor to the mouth of the Spey. I have seen a
greater number in one day off the Moy, in
Killalla Bay, than could probably now be observed
during an entire season on the southern side of
the Moray Firth.

The common hare, *Lepus timidus*, is widely
distributed throughout the lower parts of the
country, and during the autumnal months is
perhaps more numerous among the gorse-covered
wastes and peninsulas, and in the alder woods
skirting the banks of the Spey, than elsewhere.
The blue, or mountain hare, *Lepus variabilis*, is
not met with in this district, and is of unusual
occurrence even on the neighbouring heaths of
Altmoor and White Ash; while in the highlands
of Banffshire it takes the place of its congener,
and is far more common than welcome in the
deer forests of Glenfiddich and Blackwater.
When crossing the birch-clad glens and corries of
the former, the ever-watchful roe, *Cervus capreo-
lus*, will occasionally spring up in the path of the
stalker, but that animal is so thinly distributed

in this comparatively open country as seldom to
interrupt his sport. Its favourite haunts are in
the fir forests and plantations, and it is perhaps
nowhere more numerous than in the great woods
near Gordon Castle, from which, alas! the red
deer, *Cervus elaphus*, has latterly been extirpated.
From time immemorial these monarchs of the
race had dwelt among the primæval pines that
stretch away in the direction of Keith, and many
a stirring event, besides the report of a rifle, must
have varied the monotony of their domestic lives.
In the library of Gordon Castle, suspended from
the ceiling, are the skulls of two stags, with the
tynes of the antlers still inextricably locked
together,* just as when they were discovered in
fatal conflict, by one of the keepers, at the bottom
of a deep gorge through which the burn of
Fochabers pursues its earlier course. One was
already dead, the brow antler of his more powerful antagonist having transfixed his neck and
severed the jugular vein. Besides these, some of
the finest " heads " in Scotland were formerly
obtained in this locality, and adorn the walls of
the same apartment; but these golden days were
drawing to a close. In 1849 the fatal edict was

---

* This incident is alluded to by Mr. Scrope in his *Days of
Deer-stalking*, page 15.

issued by the late Duke of Richmond. The work of extermination commenced, and was so effectually carried out that before long the sole surviving stag, like "the Last of the Mohicans," disappeared from his native woods. Although formerly the number of the red deer was regularly augmented during the winter months by recruits from the distant forests of Glenfiddich and Blackwater, not even a stray visitor is now ever known to make his appearance there, which may be attributable either to the complete extirpation of the original stock—probably the chief attraction to their Highland brethren—or to the great improvement iu the pasture that has since taken place in the hill forests. Long narrow strips of the heather are annually burned in different spots, and in the following year a crop of verdant grass springs up, affording ample pasturage to the herds, as evinced not only by the greater weight of the stags themselves, but by the increased development of their antlers. Indeed it is only during exceptionally severe seasons that they now find any inducement to wander, or suffer from privation, as in the memorable winter of 1865–66, when, after the melting of the snow, an unhappy family, consisting of thirty-four red deer, one fox, and nine grouse, were discovered in the bottom of a corrie, where they had been either frozen to death or smothered in a drift. Truly " misery makes one acquainted with strange bed-fellows."

SPEY FLIES AND WADING GEAR.

———◆———

" Nec minus atque alios fallet tibi dædala musca
Artifici distincta manu plumâque tenellâ
Consita."

JAMES PARKE (Lord Wensleydale),
Cambridge Tripos Verses, 1802.

THE golden period of sport for the angler on this
portion of the Spey is from the 26th of August
to the 15th of October. On the former day the
nets are taken off, and on the latter the rod-fish-
ing season closes. The pools during the early
part of September generally contain a fair supply
of newly-run salmon and grilse, although the dry
weather which prevails at this time of year on
the Morayshire coast seldom fails to affect the
depth of the water injuriously, and to confine the
fish too much to their respective quarters, until
the first welcome autumnal spate sets them free.
The tenants of the lower pools then move higher
up the river, and shoals of fine salmon that have
long been congregating outside the estuary, and

anxiously watching an opportunity of quitting
the sea, now cross the bar and occupy all the
favourite haunts in considerable numbers.   When
the river has settled down after a real effective
flood of this sort during September, good sport
may be anticipated until the end of the season,
and a second spate is rather to be deprecated
than desired; for although it never fails to bring
up fresh recruits from the sea, yet the same
instinct that prompts these to enter the river
equally induces those it already contains to move
higher up the stream, and during their change of
quarters success is out of the question, for a
"travelling" fish never takes the fly.

It is a fact that this portion of the Spey—the
last ten or twelve miles of its course—affording
such good sport during the autumn, is totally un-
productive to the angler when the river opens
again in the spring, and for some time afterwards.
The salmon are there sure enough, and are netted
in considerable numbers, but they are all "travelling."

Fly-fishing is then hopeless, and success cannot be expected nearer than Arndilly or Aberlour:
higher up it is still better, though as the year
advances these conditions are gradually reversed.
Salmon, as a rule, generally become scarcer on

the approach of summer, while, on the other hand,
the great influx of grilse commences about the
same time.   In August, the heavier fish begin to
reappear, increasing in weight as the year progresses, and the grilse sensibly diminish in numbers; but it is not until after the 26th of August,
when the nets are removed, that the fly-fisher on
the lower waters finds everything in his favour,
and may then fairly consider himself on the best
part of the Spey.

Notwithstanding the flood of light that has
been thrown of late years on the biography of the
salmon by patient observers and zealous piscicul-
turists, how much still remains unknown and
obscure ! If any long-disputed point has latterly
been more satisfactorily settled than another, it is
that the parr, the samlet, the grilse, and the
salmon are really but one and the same fish at
different periods of its existence; yet, but a few
years ago, one of our most distinguished ichthyo-
logists assured me that the parr was a distinct
species.   Warned by the errors into which even
scientific luminaries may occasionally fall when
dealing summarily with questions so full of difficulties, I shall avoid every " *quæstio vexata* " connected with the history of *Salmo salar;* but in
reference to the fact to which I have just alluded,

and which appears to many persons so mysterious
and unaccountable, I venture to think the solu-
tion simple enough.

Assuming the correctness of the generally received opinion, that all salmon enter fresh waters
for the same purpose, and are impelled by no
other instinct to leave the sea than the desire
of ultimately depositing their ova in the gravelly
shallows of their native rivers, we may surely
conclude that these early fish are "told off" by a
never-erring Providence to occupy at a future
time the upper spawning-beds, and, having a long
journey before them, are "travelling" on their
way to the higher portions of the river, in obedience to that first law of Nature, "Increase and
multiply."

Spey flies, properly so-called, are simple and
unassuming both in composition and appearance,
yet they are tied with as much skill and care by
the best native artists as is exhibited in the fabri-
cation of the most complicated, gaudy lures, formerly imported from Ireland, but now equally
well known on the Shannon and the Tweed, and
many other Scottish as well as Norwegian rivers.
It is true that, of late years, some of these showy
strangers have been introduced here, and under
certain conditions of sky and water are found

more effective than any of the aboriginal type,
but, as a general rule, I have found that newly-
run fish in the lower waters are more readily captured with flies of the modest native pattern than
with the most brilliant exotics that can be pro-
duced by a combination of humming-bird, blue
and yellow macaw, orange-breasted toucan and
the variegated metallic plumage of the golden
pheasant.

The term "fly" is clearly a misnomer. No
insect that ever winged the air bears the slightest
resemblance to any of these artificial lures, and
even if it did, the motion imparted to the latter
under water would be unnatural and impossible.
They are evidently taken by the salmon for some
of the numerous varieties of *crustacea*—prawns,
shrimps, &c.—which, with *echinodermata*—star-
fish, &c.—constitute his rich repast in the depths
of the ocean. A conviction of the accuracy of
this surmise forced itself upon me a few years
ago, while lying down on the bank of a small
clear pool, at the tail of a rush of water through
one of the lesser arches of Spey bridge, near
Fochabers, and attentively watching the motions
of a fly at the end of a long line thrown by a
young friend of mine—an accomplished fisherman—from over the parapet above. Its undulat-

ing movements under water exactly resembled those of a living shrimp or prawn, while the continuous play of the long soft hackles of the heron or fowl—so characteristic of the old Spey flies— imitated still more closely the actions of those small, but many-legged crustaceous animals, as I had frequently observed them in the aquarium of the Zoological Society.

Notwithstanding the subdued tone and apparent simplicity of all these Spey flies, and a certain family resemblance, if I may use the expression, that pervades them all, yet after a little practice they may be easily distinguished from each other, and however trifling and insignificant these minute differences may appear to the uninitiated, yet in the eyes of the experienced native fisherman they are of considerable importance, and when salmon are shy, success is frequently supposed to depend upon their due appreciation.

It may be hardly necessary to observe, that the component parts of each sort of fly are unaffected by its size. This varies considerably. Those which are in vogue during the spring months in the upper waters, when the river is exceedingly high and rapid and the pools unusually deep, being really enormous compared with their minute representatives which are generally found most successful in the summer months and early autumn, but much must be left to the judgment of the fisherman himself; there is no rule without an exception, and I have frequently found it necessary, after a moderate rise of the water, to employ flies twice as large as those which I had found of faultless dimensions but a few days before.

The following is a list of old Spey flies. To every fisherman on the river it will be sufficient to say that the descriptions are taken from specimens tied by that accomplished artist, Shanks, of Craigellachie, of whom Mr. Barney Maguire, if he had ever visited the Spey, might perhaps have sung :—

> There's Mister Shanks too, upon the banks too,
> Och that's the fellow that can throw a loine,
> A clever boy too, he can tie a floy too,
> For art and practice he does both comboine.

OLD SPEY FLIES.

N.B.—The dubbing—or bodies—of all these flies is composed of Berlin wool.

GOLD SPEAL.—Is generally on a large hook. Body black, with only two or three turns of very broad gold flat tinsel and with a single turn of fine silver beading between the bars of the tinsel. Red cock hackle, very soft, taken from the tail coverts of the bird. Wing, mallard.

SILVER SPEAL.—Same as above, but the flat tinsel is of silver and the beading between the bars of gold.

GOLD REEACH.—Body black with three bars of flat gold tinsel, between which are three rows of very fine gold beading. Tip of the tail sometimes finished with orange silk. Red cock hackle from the tail coverts—soft and fine—along the body of the fly. Shoulder hackle of teal or guinea-fowl. Wing, mallard.

SILVER REEACH.—Same as above, except that silver tinsel and beading are used instead of gold, and grey cock hackle along the body of the fly instead of red cock hackle.

GOLD-GREEN REEACH.—Body olive, composed of a mixture of red, green, and purple fine Berlin wool. Red cock hackle from the neck. Tinsel and beading same as in gold Reeach. Shoulder hackle and wing ditto.

SILVER-GREEN REEACH.—Same as above, but with silver tinsel and beading instead of gold.

GOLD-GREEN FLY.—Dubbing the same as in green Reeach. Three or four turns of gold tinsel, according to its width, and between each of these a single turn of orange silk. Red cock hackle. Wing, teal or grey mallard.

SILVER-GREEN FLY.—Same as above, but with silver tinsel and grey cock hackle.

The flies known as "Kings" are characterized by having alternate bars of gold and silver tinsel. No beading of any kind.

GREEN KING.—Body same as green Reeach. Alternate bars of gold and silver tinsel. Red cock hackle. Shoulder hackle, teal feather. Wing, mallard.

PURPLE KING.—Body lake colour, composed of scarlet and purple mixed. Alternate bars of gold and silver. Hackle, grey or red cock, according to fancy. Shoulder hackle, teal. Wing, mallard.

BLACK KING.—Body black. Alternate bars of gold and silver tinsel. Hackle, black cock. Shoulder hackle, guinea-fowl. Wing, mallard.

GOLD PURPLE FLY, commonly called "GOLD PURPY."—Body purple. Red cock hackle, with bars of gold tinsel. Wing, mallard.

CULDRAIN FLY.—This is generally tied on a large hook. Body black. Bars of silver tinsel, rather far apart, and between each bar two threads of silk, one orange, and one yellow. Hackle, jet-black cock. Wing, grey mallard.

GOLD HERON.—Body black, with bars of gold tinsel. Between the bars two threads of gold and silver beading. Hackle very long, of the slate-coloured *back* hackles of the heron. Wing, mallard.

BLACK HERON.—Same as the last, but instead of the slate-coloured *back* hackles of the heron, use the tips of the black feathers from the *breast* of that bird.

CARRON FLY.—Body orange, bars of silver tinsel. Hackle, black feather from the breast of the heron. Wing, mallard.

Several varieties have of late years been added, which, though modest and unassuming compared with the gaudy exotics to which I have already alluded, must still be considered innovations, partaking as they do, more or less, of the plumage of the golden pheasant; they are consequently omitted from the above list, which professes to be nothing but a brief descriptive catalogue of old Spey flies.

Certain of my sporting friends have suggested that I should introduce into some part of this little book my opinion of the relative merits and disadvantages of the usual wading costumes, the result of personal experience, and especially in connection with a subject respecting which a wide-spread popular error still exists.

Whatever modifications these waterproof garments may exhibit, according to the taste or ingenuity of the various makers, it will be sufficient for my purpose to class them under two heads, viz., long boots, or stockings, pulled up separately on each leg and extending above the knee or nearly as high as the hip, and secondly, complete Macintosh trowsers—or overalls—in one piece, reaching as high as the waist, or, better still, up to the armpits, over a jersey vest, where they are usually tightened by a running string or tape, and kept in position by short braces over the shoulders. Coat and waistcoat are of course dispensed with in this costume.

Dismissing the Macintosh stockings from our consideration, as they possess but one merit—lightness or portability—let us confine our attention to the long boots and the trowsers.

The boots may be made of thick leather, such as are worn by all professional herring-fishers, or of thinner waterproof material of the same kind, or—best of all in my opinion—of vulcanized india-rubber externally, down to the ankle, the feet of thick cowhide, and the whole lined throughout with soft, flexible leather.

The great advantage of these boots consists in their excessive warmth. They should be very large and capacious, especially in the feet, so as to admit of the introduction of horsehair soles at the bottom, and, if necessary, two pair of long, thick worsted stockings, pulled over the legs of a pair of ordinary tweed trowsers. Fortified in this way, I have repeatedly waded for hours in rapid streams, when the temperature of the water was freezing, from melted snow, without experiencing the slightest chilliness or inconvenience.

When the sides of a stream or pool, along which it is desirable to wade, are known beforehand, or in ordinary shallows, these boots will answer all purposes, and are exceedingly comfortable and convenient, but where it is important to advance into deeper water, with an uncertain footing among slippery conical rocks below, to reach a goodly salmon that has been rising at a tantalizing distance; or when making a voyage of discovery among the labyrinthian mazes of the last three miles of the Spey, which perhaps have been unexplored since their creation by the recent heavy spates; and especially if dealing with a strong runaway fish struggling hard to return to the ocean which he has just left, and threatening every moment to break the single gut and tiny hook that constitute the only connection between you and him, during which exciting process you have probably to cross several rapids, without much time to select the shallowest spots,—then I say that the Macintosh trowsers are to be preferred to the boots, and that the use of the latter may occasionally, even to a good swimmer, be attended with considerable risk.

Although I had frequently been "swamped" on such occasions, when crossing rapids, yet I had hitherto always managed to get ashore without any greater inconvenience than a good ducking, and I had yet to realize the danger of wearing long boots when out of my depth. One afternoon, however, I was engaged with a very heavy fish under circumstances nearly similar to those described at page 21, but the incident to which I am now referring, occurred during the previous year. The stream was strong, the tackle delicate, and the fly exceedingly minute, so that "give and take" was the only policy likely to be successful. I had already crossed two streams that intercepted me from the main current, down which the salmon was rushing, when I came upon a third, running in at right angles to the latter, and certainly not more than thirty feet wide, which it was, of course, necessary to cross. The shingle on the near shore sloped away most invitingly, and although the opposite bank looked a little steep as I threw a hurried glance across, yet at that moment I never anticipated any difficulty in reaching it. When about half way over, however, I found myself suddenly out of my depth, holding up my rod with one hand, and with the other trying to assist my over-weighted legs in swimming across—a far more arduous task than I had imagined. Arrived there, however, I found that my troubles had only just begun. I struggled in vain to climb the perpendicular side. I felt as if a ton weight was fastened to each leg, and at last, after repeated exertions, became so exhausted that, with a sudden consciousness of immediate danger, I dropped the rod, held on with both hands at the edge of the bank, and once more strained every effort to ascend. All in vain: so throwing myself on my back, I succeeded in swimming with the greatest difficulty to the opposite shore, and felt not a little thankful when I reached it again in safety.

The sequel of this adventure will probably astonish the reader as much as it surprised myself at the time. Getting rid quickly of my water-logged boots, and throwing off my coat, I swam again across the stream and ran along the side of the river in search of my lost rod. The current had carried it down to the head of a shallow rapid, where, partially anchored by the weight of the reel near the butt, the top joint was still visible above the surface, nodding encouragingly in its gradual descent, and with tightened line, showing that the fish was still there. Well—"to make a long story short," as they say in the fairy tales—I recovered my rod, and ultimately succeeded in landing a newly-run twenty-seven pounder. He was, fortunately, hooked through the tongue, and however elated at his capture, I certainly felt at that moment that it was due rather to good luck than to good management.

The Macintosh overalls, it is true, cannot resist the low temperature of the water so effectually as the vulcanized india-rubber boots, but their great superiority consists in enabling the wearer to wade much farther into the river; in fact, breast high, and even in the event of his being carried off his legs by the force of the stream and getting out of his depth, he will find himself, if he has been used to swim in his clothes, more at home than in any ordinary garments. I am aware that this is contrary to the received opinion, but *experto crede*. I have more than once put it to the proof, and only last year convinced several incredulous friends who accompanied me on purpose to Speyside, by swimming, diving, and floating for nearly a quarter of an hour in a perfect Macintosh equipment, including a pair of heavy brogues on my feet.

The popular belief is, that if a person gets out of his depth when wearing this waterproof apparatus, the air contained in the legs of the trowsers raises them suddenly to the surface, his head and shoulders instantly sink, and he is quickly drowned; but, assuming that the dress is properly arranged, this can only occur in cases where the fisherman is unable to swim, or where, if he has never practised swimming in his clothes, the startling novelty of his situation causes him to "lose his head," or, in other words, his presence of mind. He cries out for help, and in doing so, exhausts the air in his chest, when, naturally, the skull and thorax becoming the heaviest parts of his person, his position is quickly reversed, and every subsequent attempt at inhalation fills his lungs still more with water, and all is soon over. Many fatal instances of this kind have occurred which, of course, have only served to propagate the popular error, but I am inclined to think that the neglect of a very simple precaution, on the importance of which it is impossible to dwell too strongly, has been the chief cause of loss of life in all cases where the sufferers were known to have been previously able to swim.

I soon found that the running string, or tape, attached to the trowsers for the purpose of tightening them round the chest, was not sufficiently close-fitting to exclude the water from forcing an entrance in the event of total immersion. I therefore tried a leather strap in addition, well buckled up, but it became relaxed when saturated, and after various experiments I found that a strong hempen whip-cord was the very thing required, as it contracted perceptibly when wet, and, with the addition of a second round the waist, rendered everything quite secure. I could then swim for ten minutes at a time without the intrusion of more than about a wineglassful of water, which gradually forced its way through the circumference of the flannel jersey, however tightly compressed by the cords. The well-nailed leather brogues, so far from inconveniently impeding the floating power, acted merely as a slight counterpoise to the partially inflated and buoyant overalls, and the satisfactory result was simply a greater facility in keeping above water than I had often previously experienced when practising swimming in a loose flannel suit, or light tweed garments especially selected for the occasion.

A BLANK DAY IN A DEER-FOREST.

———◆———

"Nature teaches beasts to know their friends."
SHAKSPEARE.

THE more I see of the red deer in their native forests, the more I feel interested in their ways and habits. Indeed, almost every stalk, whether successful or otherwise, affords me some opportunity of admiring that ceaseless watchfulness on the part of the hinds, without the exercise of which the fat and comparatively lazy stags would less frequently escape the rifle.

During the excitement of my first season, the paramount object was, naturally enough, to compass the death of the animal I was in quest of; and it was not until the novelty of the sport had in some measure worn away, after the acquisition of several good "heads," that I began to derive new pleasure from observing the frequent examples of their marvellous instinct.

Besides the acute sense of smell with which these animals are endowed, enabling them to detect the slightest taint in the air to the windward of their position, they possess other gifts in a remarkable degree, by the exercise of which they succeed in avoiding danger, and this frequently at the very moment when escape would appear to be most improbable.

Foremost among these is their power of recognizing the sound, or cry, of alarm uttered by various native birds of the forest, and of appreciating the difference between this and the ordinary voice or call-note of the species. There would seem to be no link of attachment between the animal that confers and the one that receives the benefit, which appears to me to characterize the exercise of this faculty in the red deer and to distinguish the case itself from others which at first sight might appear to be analogous.

The author of that charming book, "The Monasteries of the Levant," had the enviable good fortune, while stalking a crocodile on the banks of the Nile, to corroborate the accuracy of Herodotus's account of a singular episode in its biography, which for upwards of two thousand years had been looked upon as apocryphal. When within a few yards of the sleeping monster, and just as he was preparing to pull the trigger, his attention was attracted by a bird about the size of a plover, walking up and down near the crocodile. Suddenly springing up, and uttering its cry of "zic-zac "—by which name it is known in Egypt*—it flew several times against his head and face, to give the alarm, and so successfully, that before the narrator of the adventure could fire, he was covered with mud dashed over him by the great reptile as he rushed into the river. Herodotus's account is as follows. " I proceed now to describe the nature of the crocodile . . . . Living in the water its throat is always full of leeches : beasts and birds universally avoid it, the trochilus alone excepted, which from a sense of gratitude it treats with kindness. When the crocodile leaves the water, it reclines itself in the sand—and generally towards the west—with its mouth open ; the trochilus entering its throat destroys the leeches ; in acknowledgment for which service it never does the trochilus injury." †

Geoffry St. Hilaire admits the fact, but says that "the bird enters the mouth of the crocodile attracted, not by leeches, but by a small insect like

* The zic-zac is the τροχίλος of Herodotus and the *Charadrius Ægyptiacus* of modern ornithologists.
† BELOE'S *Herodotus.*

a gnat." * At any rate it can no longer be doubted that a link of attachment between the two creatures does exist, and that in all probability the bird is in the habit of feeding on the small flies and numerous aquatic insects either adhering to the crocodile itself or exposed on the slimy surface of the mud during his passage from the water, and admitting at the same time the truth of Rochefoucault's celebrated definition of gratitude, there can be no difficulty in believing that the zic-zac is prompted by selfish interest to keep watch over the huge saurian who supplies him with such a well-furnished larder, and habitually to act as his sentinel on those occasions.

Another instance of this kind is mentioned in Gordon Cumming's "Sports of Southern Africa." Here the rhinoceros enacts the part of the crocodile, and is carefully tended by a swarm of little birds, of the starling family, who accompany him on all occasions, performing the same duties for him, when asleep, that the zic-zac fulfils for the crocodile; screaming and fluttering, and dashing at his eyes on the slightest approach of danger : but their motives are evidently not disinterested, for when unalarmed they may be seen continually feeding on the parasitic insects that

* See also Bishop STANLEY's *Familiar History of Birds.*

infest his skin, or on the flies that perpetually buzz about his ears and head. So faithful, indeed, is their allegiance, that they adhere pertinaciously to the back of the rhinoceros, when in full retreat, and instead of deserting him as he rushes through the trees, or under the boughs, they merely dodge to the opposite side of his body, or creep under his belly, maintaining their hold with their claws until the danger has passed away, when they resume their position on his back. In this case even the most sceptical must admit that the services of the bird to the object of its care are not gratuitous, and it seems to furnish presumptive evidence that the attachment of the zic-zac to the crocodile is of a similar nature.

Now for my own experience of an analogous case.

Many years ago, in the west of Ireland, where I served my youthful apprenticeship to every wild sport that the British Islands can afford—except deer-stalking—I used to vary the salmon and trout-fishing, during the summer, by an occasional seal-shooting expedition on the sandhills and islands outside the river Moy, in Killalla Bay. At low tides, when these banks were left uncovered, great numbers of seals used to crawl up the slopes of the lesser islets and indulge in a sound slumber, in full enjoyment of the warm sunshine. It was impossible to get within rifle-shot in an open row-boat, as the sound of the oars, even when muffled, soon reached their ears and alarmed them. Now and then, while I was mackerel-fishing in a sailing-boat, a seal would perhaps indiscreetly raise his head out of the water within thirty yards, and as I always kept a rifle ready for such a chance, I occasionally succeeded in bagging one after a long chase, the first shot rarely proving fatal, although sufficiently severe, perhaps, to compel the animal to reappear on the surface in less time than if he had not been badly wounded. Then commenced a chase in the row-boat, the seal repeatedly diving, but each time remaining for a shorter period under water, until at last I could get near enough to shoot him through the head, while the man in the bow would endeavour, though not always successfully, to secure the prize with the boat-hook before it sank lifeless under the surface.

Far different tactics were necessary when trying to circumvent the seals as they dozed on the sandbanks. Watching until the tide had more than half retired, and always before the ebb, I used to conceal myself in a light, shallow, flat-bottomed punt, where I lay on my face, covered with sea-

weed, a rifle projecting from one end and a paddle
from the other, the occasional use of the latter
enabling me, without any noise, to keep the little
craft from turning round, although entirely pro-
pelled by the receding tide. Occasionally I could
succeed in getting within shot, if the slumberers
happened to be unattended by a great black-backed
gull, *Larus marinus;* but that was a rare event. A
bird of this species, and one only at a time, generally
stood near them, and no sentinel ever kept more
faithful watch. As soon as I used to perceive him I
knew that all chance of bagging a seal was over for
that day. He was a capital judge too of distance,
for he would stand patiently, and quite immovable,
on one leg, apparently regardless of the object
that was gradually nearing the banks, or pretend-
ing not to see it, until I was almost within shot,
when suddenly he would rise, and flying round and
round over the seals, alarm them at once, uttering
all the time his loud, taunting laugh. Turning
rapidly " right about face " they would hobble
down the bank and soon disappear in the water,
while their protector, not satisfied with having
baulked me of my sport, would keep at a safe
distance over my head, and, adding insult to
injury, continue to repeat his jeering notes, until
at last they gradually died away in the distance.

I have frequently found fragments of salmon
and different species of sea-fish on isolated rocks
and sandbanks in various parts of the bay; doubtless the remains of many a repast left by the
seals, and duly appreciated by their grateful attendant.   The number of grilse and salmon taken
with the fly—as well as net—exhibiting severe
wounds from the paws and teeth of the seals, is
well known, but it is insignificant, compared with
the quantity devoured by them; while many
others, again, escape for the moment, only to die
ultimately of these injuries, before they can ascend
the stream; and as, after the commencement of de-
composition, their bodies soon float on the surface
of the ocean, they furnish a plentiful supply of food
for this large gull, who, being unable to dive, is in
fact nothing better than a marine scavenger.
Doubtless he fully appreciates the important
services rendered to him by the seals, and it is
quite reasonable to suppose that he is not in-
fluenced by disinterested motives in acting as
their guardian angel.

Between the red deer and his feathered friends
there would seem to be no such tender tie.   His
instantaneous appreciation of any sound or
movement on their part, indicating the slightest
suspicion of approaching danger to themselves,

appears to be the result of hereditary instinct aided by acute observation. These reflections have been forced upon me by the experience of a single day's stalking in Glenfiddich forest last week. Everything looked favourable on that morning as I left the lodge with the forester, McKay, attended by his brother John, the gillie, leading the two deer hounds. A steady breeze, neither too light nor too strong, was blowing right down the glen from the south-west; the day was perhaps occasionally a little. too bright, as the sun every now and then peeped out from the grey clouds, but we expected no difficulty in finding deer, especially as a large herd had been alarmed on the previous evening in the adjoining forest of Blackwater, and had been seen to cross over the ridge of Cook's Cairn to the upper part of Glen-fiddich, in which direction we were now proceeding.

After following the course of the stream on the right bank for a couple of miles, we halted, and examining with our glasses the sides of the corries opposite, we soon discovered several small herds, consisting principally of hinds, and the few stags that were among them did not seem, to the experienced eye of the forester, sufficiently tempting, either by spread of horn or size of body, to induce us to think more about them. After another half-hour's walking we again came to a halt, and reconnoitred the sides of the hills in all directions. There was one steep corrie on our left, through the centre of which a burn ran down in the direction of the river. A few birch-trees fringed its sides, intermixed with occasional fragments of rock, while still higher up, large patches of bright green, where the heather had been burned and the grass had recently grown, afforded a beautiful contrast in colour to the wider extent of purple in which they seemed to be embedded. In the midst of one of these verdant spots we soon made out several deer, some graz-ing, others lying down, and scattered here and there at a distance from the main body, several hinds higher up the hill, and a few others close to the birches near the banks of the burn.

I soon perceived that there were about half a dozen stags among them, and at least two with fine heads. This was encouraging, but on looking round to the forester, who had just shut up his glass, I knew at once from the expression of his countenance that he did not share my sanguine expectations. One, he admitted, that was lying down, was a "grand beast" with a royal head. He recognized him at once, having stalked him in

vain last season two or three times. On the
present occasion the position of the hinds was
the cause of his anxiety. Most of them were
grazing on the other side of this stag, from which
direction alone we could venture to approach them,
as the wind was blowing right up the corrie.
They might perhaps move lower down in the
direction of the river a little later in the day, and
as such a chance as this was not likely to occur
often, we decided on continuing our course up
the main glen for a considerable distance, and
after crossing the Fiddich, that we should ascend
the opposite hill, climb the ridge overlooking
Blackwater forest, and then, turning back, keep
the heights a little above us on our left, until by
this circuitous route we had arrived opposite the
head of the corrie in which the deer were grazing.
This would ultimately bring us to leeward of
them, and at the same time afford the best chance
of getting within shot of the big stag in the event
of the hinds and the rest of the herd moving
lower down, and that we could succeed in crawling
over the bare ridge of the hill and reach the commencement of the burn unobserved by them.

We had already carried out almost half of this
programme ; had crossed the stream a couple of
miles higher up, and were toiling through a small

corrie, with the intention of emerging from it at the
other end, over the crest of the hill, when McKay,
who was leading, suddenly stopped, and dropping
on his knees, motioned to me to lie down—the
gillie with the dogs, of course doing the same.
On creeping up to him I found that he had got a
glimpse of a stag grazing on the hill to our right.
We had nothing to conceal us but the heather,
which, however, grew thickly near the course of
the burn, so crawling through it, in snake-like
fashion, we at last got within about three hundred
yards of him.   Then I ventured to look.   There
he was : grazing leisurely : a beautiful broadside
shot : standing off distinctly from the dark background.   He had a fair head, of ten points, and
appeared in capital condition.   Not another
animal of his own species was within sight.
Several tussocks covered with mosses and lichens
rose within rifle range of him, and once there, I
could hardly fail of killing him.   Indeed at that
moment I felt certain of success, as the intervening ground was well furnished with heather, and
we had already overcome the chief difficulties in
reaching our present position.   Quickly resuming
our task, we had accomplished about a quarter of
the distance, when a cock grouse sprang up, right
in front of McKay, and flew back over our heads,

down the corrie, quite away from the stag,
uttering all the time his loud, half-crowing, half-
screaming cry of alarm.   Looking up at the same
instant I had the mortification of seeing the
deer bounding away at his best pace up the hill,
and could only gaze helplessly at him until he
disappeared over the brow.   As for the forester,
this was too usual an occurrence to disturb his
characteristic equanimity, or to elicit any audible
demonstration of feeling on his part.

   We had still the big stag in prospect, and
another hour brought us over the ridge and round
the hills to the top of the corrie in which we had
seen him and the herd of deer that accompanied
him.   How my guide hit off the place where it
was necessary for us to halt and crawl up the
slope to our left, seemed marvellous to me, but
when on the summit itself I saw at a glance that
he had conducted me to the very spot, although
I could discover no landmark of any kind that
could have assisted him.   Here we slowly raised
our heads, and noiselessly opening our glasses
examined the sides of the corrie.   There was
"the muckle hart," still lying down, and we saw
that most of the hinds we had previously observed
between him and our present position had fortunately grazed nearer the river on either side of

him, so that if we could only get over the first
thirty or forty yards of the crest of the hill, which
was naked and slaty, without being observed, we
might reach the burn and some birch-trees, after
which the banks, although low, would suffice to
screen us from the hinds as we crawled through
the bed of the stream. Leaving the gillie, therefore, and the dogs at the other side, we commenced
operations by turning over on our backs and half-
sliding, half-wriggling, feet foremost, down the
steep incline, we successfully accomplished this,
the most difficult part of our task, and then
commenced crawling over the stones in the bed of
the burn, every now and then immersed in a pool
of water, as the banks were still too low to admit
even of a stooping posture. At last we gained
the friendly shelter of the birch-trees, and rising
to our feet, advanced with comparatively little
difficulty until we reached the base of a naked
elevated mound overhanging the bed of the stream,
which afforded an opportunity of ascertaining our
exact position. Slow and stealthy was our progress as we crept up to the ridge of the rough
slope, when I ventured, as cautiously as possible,
to peep into the glen below. It was a magnificent
sight. There, within three hundred yards of me,
was the big stag, still lying down, but with his

head turned away from us. Even when thus foreshortened, he looked a giant among the others, two or three of whom, as well as several hinds, were grazing on either side of him. The wind too was all right, and McKay urged that no time should be lost in backing out of our present position as cautiously as we had reached it, and after returning by our former track to the burn, that we should crawl down it again as far as a stunted birch-tree on the same side of the bank, not more than two hundred yards off, under cover of which I could get a broadside shot at the stag when he rose from his lair and commenced feeding. Before retiring, however, I could not help throwing one more admiring glance on the landscape below. The lofty hill of Corryhabbie, and beyond this the still higher Ben Rennis, with white clouds capping its summit, rose at the opposite side of Glenfiddich, while a limited view of the middle distance, immediately in front, was bounded to the right and left by the sides of the corrie which in dark shadow seemed to frame the sides of the picture.

Hardly had I obtained more than a glimpse of this lovely scene when a distant croaking sound attracted my attention. I had no difficulty in recognizing it, although it was the first time I

J Wolf delt   M & N Hanhart lith

THE BLACK INFORMER

Page 93

had heard it in a deer forest, and for a few moments it caused me no apprehension. Suddenly, however, the deep, hoarse notes, that at first had reached my ear at regular intervals, were followed by a succession of rapidly-repeated angry barks in a higher key. These soon became louder and louder, and turning up my eyes, I saw, to my consternation, just over our heads, a large raven. He had come over from Blackwater forest, in our rear, having probably got sight of the gillie with the dogs on the other side of the hill. Now he evidently perceived us and redoubled his warnings, swooping round and circling directly over us. In a few seconds all was over. Away went the hinds. Last of all uprose the stag himself, slowly and leisurely; at first looking round him proudly, as if disdaining to take alarm from so slight a cause, and at the same moment revealing his grand proportions and his magnificent spreading antlers. Then, having apparently made up his mind in which direction to retreat, he trotted up the side of the corrie in the track of the fugitive hinds. Presently we saw the whole herd slacken their pace and, one by one, disappear over the hill; until, at last, "the monarch of the glen" himself loomed in dark profile on the sky-line, and then vanished from our sight.

"Bad luck, that, McKay," said I, scarcely able to restrain the bitterness of my feelings. I could see that my companion fully shared them, and that this second misfortune was too much for his stoicism, for among the mysterious sounds issuing from his mouth, as he slowly inserted a consolatory quid of tobacco within its precincts, I could occasionally detect an imprecation on the head of the "doom'd corbie" that had spoiled our sport and robbed us of the finest stag in the forest.

FLOODS ON THE SPEY.

BURNSIDE POOL.

———◆———

" Th' expanded waters gather on the plain,
  They float the fields and overtop the grain :
  Then rushing onwards with a sweepy sway,
  Bear flocks and folds and labouring hinds away.
  Nor safe the dwellings were ; for sapped by floods,
  Their houses fell upon their household gods."
  DRYDEN'S *Virgil.*

" Piscium et summo genus hæsit ulmo,
  Nota quæ sedes fuerat columbis."
  HORACE.

AT this season of the year the occurrence of a
flood sufficient to overflow and devastate the cultivated fields above the banks of the Spey, is a rare
event, although I have witnessed sudden spates
after heavy falls of rain in the Highlands, during
which, the waters rose many feet in a few hours,
and fir-trees, fragments of buttresses, and débris
of all kinds, were swept down the stream ; the
round boulders and stones at the same time, as
they rolled along the sides of the river, sounding

like a continuous fusillade of distant musketry, while the whole scene enabled one to realize what the result must be when the mighty river is in earnest and rushes down in full force.

Of all the visitations of this kind that have occurred in the north of Scotland, none can compare, for extent of area and destructive effect, with the tremendous flood of the 3rd and 4th of August, 1829. Ruin and misery were indeed universal, not only on the Spey, but along the course of all the principal rivers in Morayshire, Banffshire, and a great part of Aberdeenshire. The deluge of rain that was the immediate cause of this unprecedented calamity fell chiefly on the Monadhleadh mountains, between the south-eastern portion of Loch Ness and the sources of the Findhorn, and on the Cairngorm range—part of the Grampians. The country above Kingussie would appear to have escaped, but all the cultivated ground in the neighbourhood of the Spey, from thence to the sea—a distance of seventy miles—was inundated by the waters.*

---

* A most interesting account of this memorable event was compiled soon afterwards by the late Sir T. Dick Lauder, to whose pages the reader is referred for a minute description of many a fatal struggle, heroic rescue, and hairbreadth escape, during the floods on this river and its tributaries, as well as on the Findhorn, the Nairn, the Deveron, and the Dee.

To refer only to a few examples of devastation during the last twelve or fifteen miles of its course; the district with which I am most familiar.

Near the mouth of the Fiddich—one of its principal tributaries—the upper part of which runs through the deer forest of Glenfiddich, the farm of Dandaleith was converted into a perfect desert, a great extent of rich land covered with sand and gravel, "all the corn-stacks floated off like a fleet of ships, and a thriving distillery was overwhelmed."

About five miles lower down, nearly opposite Ben Aigen, the village of Rothes, though somewhat elevated above the plain, was nearly submerged, and several substantially-built houses either partially or totally ruined; while at Orton, on the left bank of the river, below Boat o' Brig, upwards of a hundred acres of crops were destroyed, and fifty more carried away, or rendered valueless for agricultural purposes.

At the small town of Garmouth, near the mouth of the Spey, many houses of two and even three stories high were half thrown down, the whole plain, as far as the eye could reach, was covered with water, the shores of the harbour studded with stranded vessels, and even the sea-beach strewed with the carcases of animals, including "millions of dead hares and rabbits."*

But the most memorable calamity on this part of Spey was the destruction of the great bridge of Fochabers, near Gordon Castle, spanning the river on the high road between Keith and Elgin. "It consisted of four arches; two of ninety-five feet and two of seventy-five feet span each, making a total waterway of three hundred and forty feet. On the morning of the 4th of August, the entire plain, from Ben Aigen to the sea, presented one vast undulating expanse of dark brown water, in some places more than two miles broad. The floating wrecks of nature and of human industry and comfort were strewed over its surface, which was only varied by the appearance of the tufted tops of submerged trees, or by the roofs of houses, to which, in more than one instance, the miserable inhabitants were seen clinging, while boats were plying about for their relief. And still the elements raved with un-abated fury, so that not a bird could dare to wing the air."†

Several persons were on the bridge during the early part of the day, looking over the parapets at the wreck, carcases of dead animals and other

* Sir T. D. Lauder.   † Sir T. D. Lauder.   Op. cit.

bodies which were hurried through, but most of these had subsequently congregated at the Banff-shire extremity, to witness an attempt on the part of the forester and his men to protect the mound of approach, when suddenly a fissure appeared in the very centre of the path, immediately above the second arch on the Morayshire side. Those who were nearest ran for their lives, giving the alarm to others; and, a few seconds afterwards, down went the whole mass of the two arches on the left bank of the river, carrying with it a lame youth, who unfortunately had not been able to effect his escape.

For some years afterwards passengers and goods were conveyed across in boats, until an Act of Parliament in 1832 enabled the trustees to erect a single wooden arch in place of the two that were destroyed—thus dispensing with the necessity of a pier in the most rapid part of the stream. This, at the time of its erection, was the largest of that description in Britain,* but as the work showed symptoms of decay in 1853, cast iron was substituted for timber; the arch was completed in two years, and has ever since effectually resisted the force of the waters.

Although such a calamity as this terrible deluge

* Dr. Longmuir's *Speyside.*

of 1829 has not since occurred, yet the winter
torrents are generally powerful enough to overflow
the left bank of the river, and, in spite of groins,
buttresses, and other contrivances both expensive
and laborious, large gaps and chasms are frequently exposed after the subsidence of the
floods, and the work has to be commenced
anew.

For six or seven miles above Fochabers bridge,
the alluvial and comparatively flat tract, which
suffered so much, is still the site of some of the
richest and most highly-cultivated farms in this
part of Scotland, forming a remarkable contrast
to the opposite side of the river, with its precipitous sandstone cliffs and lofty hills, clothed with
pine-woods, extending into the interior in an
easterly direction.   The lands of Dipple were remarkable for their fertility, and shared a celebrity
with some others, as recorded in the following old
rhyme,—

> " Dipple, Dundurcus, Dandaleith, and Dalvey
> Are the four fairest farms on the banks of the Spey."

At Dipple there is also an ancient cemetery,
and a fish-bed was long since discovered in the
same locality, which has furnished to collectors
many fine specimens of ichthyolites, but is now

nearly exhausted. Higher up still is the farm
of Burnside, and beyond it the lands and de-
mesne of Orton.

Until a few years ago one of the best salmon-
pools in this part of Spey was at Burnside—
immediately opposite the gorge of Alt Derg at the
other side of the river. I never knew it in its
palmy days, before the annual encroachments of
the stream had gradually eaten away so much
valuable land that it became necessary at last to
undertake a serious war of defence against these
winter torrents, and to call into play all the
engineering skill and resources that were available. On such occasions, where the ground is
sufficiently firm, huge crates, strongly constructed
and filled with large boulders, are found to be the
best protection ; these, placed closely alongside of
each other and securely fastened together, constitute an admirable though expensive bulwark. On
the other hand, where the devastation is usually
greatest, the section of the bank reveals a loose
boulder clay, and a different and comparatively
economical plan of defence is adopted, but especially execrable in the eyes of a salmon-fisher.
During the heats of summer and early autumn,
when the river is at its lowest, numbers of young
trees—foliage, branches, and all—are laid down at

H

the bottom near the shore, the uppermost boughs pointing outwards, all closely packed together and forming a regular *chevaux de frise*, frequently extending far into the stream; large boulders are again heaped upon the trunks nearest the land, and then another layer of trees, the process being repeated until the work is supposed to have attained a sufficient elevation. This sort of subaqueous fence sometimes extends for a considerable distance, occasionally interrupted, only to be recommenced twenty or thirty yards lower down, and where the banks have once been subjected to this treatment, it is easy to imagine that the salmon-fisher must seek for a more favourable spot for the exercise of his art.

The year before my arrival, Burnside pool had been fortified on the above system, and consequently deserted by anglers, but I had heard so much of its former renown, and so many rumours had reached me of the number of large fish still frequenting its deep recesses in perfect security, that I felt an irresistible desire to pay it a visit and invade the sanctuary, although with a full knowledge of the consequences of such an attempt. Even partial success was of course out of the question while the water was perfectly clear and the use of single gut casting-lines and small

flies necessary; watching my opportunity, therefore, until the river had acquired a coffee-coloured
tint after a partial rise, I sallied forth one afternoon with a stiff, powerful twenty-foot rod, treble
gut and large flies specially prepared for the trial.
On reaching the spot I saw at a glance the difficulties with which I should have to contend. The
river rolled deep and dark close to the very bank,
the trunks of the trees, embedded in the boulders
below, bordered the entire extent of the pool, and
even where these were not visible I knew that the
branches of others lay treacherously beneath the
water in every direction. Wading was out of the
question. Every cast must be from the shore,
and far out too, where I could already see several
good fish rising in the most tantalizing manner.
Beyond them, a bank of shingle, commencing
much higher up, seemed to divide the river into
two branches, but the arm at the other side was
comparatively shallow, while the main stream
near me rushed over the promontory at its head
in a deep, impassable rapid, near which was an
angular buttress projecting into the river, where
I decided on commencing operations. Putting a
large spring Spey fly on the treble gut casting-
line, and testing the strength of every portion of
the latter, I threw into the stream just above

H 2

where I had seen a large fish rise several times. At the second cast I had him, and away he went directly towards the rapid, springing repeatedly out of the water—a twenty-pounder at least—then suddenly turning back he bolted across to the opposite side, still fortunately keeping away from me. All this time I had "held on like grim death," showing him the butt of the rod, but his violent plunges and strenuous efforts to descend the stream severely tried the strength of the upper joints; prudence, therefore, induced me to yield partly to his wishes, and while grudgingly giving him line, to keep him at the same time as near the surface as possible. He was still, as I thought, sufficiently far from the bank to escape the branches underneath, when, with a tremendous rush, down he went to the bottom. Sulking, thought I, as the line became fixed, and no response followed the movement of my wrist in attempting to rouse him to renewed activity. Then, shortening the line as much as possible, and exerting a strong upward pressure—trying, in fact, to lift him perpendicularly, usually a successful expedient on similar occasions—I directed my attendant gillie—it was before I had enlisted Simon—to pelt him with stones thrown from the near side, and within a foot or two of the spot

where we supposed he was lying. All in vain ;
not even a twitch was perceptible ; nothing but
the monotonous, thrilling sort of sensation that
is invariably telegraphed along the rod when the
hook is hopelessly fixed in some inanimate object
at the bottom. The awful truth then burst upon
me. He was gone ! Every attempt to extricate
the tackle was unavailing : it was evidently entangled among the branches of the trees in the
deepest part of the river, and as it was impossible to reach the spot by wading, I laid my rod
on the ground and walked down the side of the
bank in search of a fir-pole, with the assistance of
which I hoped to reach the lower portion of the
reel line, and thus sacrifice, perhaps, only the
treble gut and the fly at the extremity. While
seeking for this, I discovered, about a hundred
yards lower down, a little bay, sloping gradually
away inland, of comparatively shallow, dead water,
as it receded from the stream, quite uninfested
by boughs, boulders, or obstructions of any
kind. All this time several fish were rising in
the upper part of the pool, and not a moment was
to be lost ; so, having at last found a long branch
of a Scotch fir, I contrived with its aid to drag
out my line—losing only the gut and fly at the
end—and quickly putting on the strongest tackle

and a large hook, I recommenced operations. It was evidently one day in a hundred. I believe the fish would have risen at any lure, however coarse or rudely constructed. At the very first throw I was fast in another, and now I determined to alter my strategy, and to hurry him down stream as quickly as possible, in hopes of reaching the little harbour of dead water before anything untoward should occur, fully prepared, of course, for the hold of the fly giving way, but dreading far more the alternative of the line becoming entangled in the trees which, I was now aware, extended far into the bed of the pool; so raising his head above water I allowed him to lash about furiously for a short time, and then, before he had made up his mind in what direction to bolt, I urged him rapidly down stream, running along the bank, but keeping well in front of him, and with a short line forcing him away by the power of the rod, while the gillie, with a battery of stones which he continued to discharge at intervals, tried to frighten him as much as possible from the submerged branches at the side. All this time I saw that fish were still rising above me, and I determined, whatever the result might be, to make short work of it, so, reversing my rod, reel upwards, to alter the strain, and again

" showing him the butt," I fairly dragged him along until just opposite the inlet of calm water, and at last steered my prize, now nearly exhausted, into the welcome haven, where, after a few ineffectual efforts to return to the stream, he was easily clipped; an eighteen-pounder, in prime condition, and as bright as silver. He was hooked through the tongue, and landed in less time than I have taken to describe the particulars of his capture, and as the numerous plunges in the upper part of the pool showed that the fish still continued in a taking humour—all large salmon, not a grilse among them—I was soon trying for another, and in a few minutes repeating the experiment that had lately proved successful, and again at close quarters with a heavy fish. Already had I got him half-way down the pool when suddenly the fly lost its hold, the rod became bolt upright and he bade me farewell. The fourth encounter ended in a capture, and I was equally fortunate with the fifth, both being firmly hooked, but I lost the sixth very much after the manner of the first, in trying to force him to the surface during the early part of the engagement; he being too wilful or too strong to submit to such severe discipline; for suddenly turning directly towards me he plunged into the *chevaux de frise* close to the bank and quickly dissolved our brief partnership.

The shades of evening were now beginning to fall, and it was time to start for home. I had three good fish, however, to take with me as trophies, and received many congratulations on my success, though I must confess to having felt half ashamed at being compelled to attribute it to tactics less worthy of the noble art than of the deep-sea practice of a professional cod-fisher.

TYNET BURN AND ITS ICHTHYOLITES.

—◆—

"Forthwith the sounds and seas, each creek and bay
    With fry innumerable swarm, and shoals
    Of fish, that with their fins and shining scales
    Glide under the green wave . . . ."
                                        Paradise Lost.

"The tender soil then stiff'ning by degrees,
    Shut from the bounded earth the bounding seas."
                                        DRYDEN'S *Virgil.*

IN one of the long corridors at Gordon Castle
connecting the central or more ancient part of
the building with the wings, are placed two small
glazed cabinets similar to those containing coins
or mineralogical specimens in a public museum.
They stand opposite to each other, immediately
under two of the windows that light this passage,
and a better situation for displaying their contents could not have been selected.   Nevertheless,
so closely are the walls on either side studded
with the skulls and antlers of stags grimly looking down on the passer-by as he proceeds to the

circular gallery at the western extremity—where
these trophies of the deer-stalker, reaching all round
to the very ceiling, form a perfect Golgotha—that
the cabinets and their contents might easily
escape his observation. Yet to a student of fossil
ichthyology, or I may even say to a lover of
nature like myself, but "skin-deep" in the
science, this small collection is most interesting,
and doubly so from its having been procured in
the immediate neighbourhood. It was formed by
Mr. Arthur Lennox, a talented young geologist,
but a few years ago, during a summer visit here,
and consists of calcareous nodules of various sizes,
which, after having been split longitudinally, exhibit in the centre of each section a more or less
perfect representation, in profile, of a fish of the
old red sandstone—the formation developed in
this neighbourhood. The nodule, or *matrix*, containing each is generally elliptical, that is to say,
of an oval form, but depressed instead of being
round, and when these are discovered in the
shallow stratum or fish-bed, are found lying on
their flat sides. They are of a drab colour, while
the fossils themselves that are imbedded in them
appear of a ferruginous Indian red, occasionally
tinged with purple, and thus the outline of the
latter is the more distinct from the contrast of its

deep warm colour to the light tint of the framework in which it is set.

Hugh Miller, the first great explorer of the old red sandstone formation in Scotland, whose charming descriptions are probably unsurpassed in power and eloquence, conjectures that after the burial of the fish in a soft muddy sediment, the chemical influence of the decaying animal matter deposited the lime with which it was charged, and hence the calcareous nodules in which we find their remains enclosed. Probably the putrefying bodies of the fish might have possessed a similar power of attracting to themselves the oxide of iron from the surrounding mass of ferruginous sand.

Although I had previously seen a few similar specimens in public museums, yet I confess that they never excited in me more than a temporary interest, or passing feeling of admiration—the rival charms of the huge reptiles of the Oolite or the gigantic mammalia of the Tertiary epoch, although comparatively recent, soon distracting my attention—but under what different circumstances was I now examining them ! The old red sandstone actually surrounded me, its great antiquity forcing itself more than ever on the imagination. Nothing beneath me, between it and the prepalæozoic non-fossiliferous rocks, but the Silurian deposits with their corals, molluscs and crustacea. All subsequent periods unrepresented, though each had its fauna and flora and lasted for millions of years! Palæozoic, Mesozoic, Cainozoic: all passed away without leaving behind a trace of their existence. The coal-seams and compact limestones of the carboniferous age; the coloured sandstones and magnesian limestones of Permia; the salt deposits of the Trias; the reptilian bearing beds of the oolite; the marine fauna of the chalk; the more modern strata of the tertiaries and post-tertiaries! Can we wonder if the human mind is bewildered in endeavouring to realize the duration of these accumulated ages? Driven to the very extremity of the abyss of thought, it has sometimes seemed to me that the philosophical sentiment of the Roman poet might often apply to the modern student of the world's history,—

"Quæsivit cœlo lucem, ingemuitque repertâ."

Yet it is a matter of strict scientific demonstration that the time which has elapsed since the first appearance of man on this earth up to the present moment is absolutely insignificant when compared with the interval between that event and the period when these red sandstone fishes peopled the waters of the Old World.

Perhaps the most wonderful circumstance connected with these ichthyolites is the preservation of their external form. A good specimen, in fact, represents a picture of the animal itself coloured in light red, Indian red, or occasionally varied with Vandyke brown on a grey background, carefully executed, and with many of the details far more minutely finished than if it were an illustration for a modern work on the natural history of fishes. The same peculiarity applies to each in a greater or less degree, while among the fossil fish of the chalk and of subsequent formations, instead of this *portrait*, as it were, of each, the bones alone are usually in a state of preservation, and the ichthyolite is represented by a skeleton. I will endeavour to explain this as familiarly and concisely as I can. All the fish of the old red sandstone epoch were cartilaginous. Those of subsequent formations were principally osseous—or bony—as are with few exceptions the fish of the present day. The skeleton of the cartilaginous fishes is composed of gristle ; mere animal matter without the addition of the calcareous earth that constitutes bone. It was therefore liable to rapid decay, but as if to

compensate for this, their external covering was
like a coat of armour. Their bones in fact were
outside, sometimes in the form of broad plates, at
others in a beautiful arrangement of closely-fitting
scales, all coated with enamel. This will account
for the preservation of the external form. The head,
as in osseous fishes, is of bone, but unlike the latter,
which is divided into a great number of distinct
parts, it generally consisted of a single piece
without any joint. It was therefore less liable to
decay, or at least to separation from the body, and
yet among the specimens in this collection, and
in those I subsequently procured myself in the
fish-bed of Tynet burn, the skull was decidedly
the least perfect portion of each, although in
many species it would appear to have been protected by a continuation of the enamelled armour.

But the most striking distinction between the
cartilaginous and the ordinary osseous fishes, is in
the form of the tail. The latter, as you know,
like the salmon, herring, cod, or mackerel, and
even the flat turbot or sole, possess a tail composed of two equal parts; set on, as it were, at
the *end* of the vertebral column. Not so among
the cartilaginous fishes. With them it is formed
on both the upper and lower portion of the spine.
In fact, the body, gradually attenuated as it

approaches the extremity, seems at last to pass through the two portions of the tail, which is invariably much more largely developed on the under than on the upper side, so as almost to appear crooked and ill formed. Have you ever seen a shark or a dog-fish? They are modern examples of the cartilaginous series; so is the sturgeon; and in all these the unequally lobed form of tail prevails, although not to such an extent as in these ancient fishes, in some of which indeed the upper portion of the caudal fin is even absent altogether.

One specimen in this collection, totally dissimilar as it was from all the others, attracted my attention immediately. The *pterichthys*—or winged fish. If I had never perused Hugh Miller's pages, I should hardly have supposed it to be a fish at all. It had more the characters of a crustacean or chelonian animal, to my inexperienced eyes; the body being covered with plates closely fitting, like those of a lobster or tortoise. Although smaller, it seems to be a more perfect example than that from which Miller—its first discoverer —took his description, the round head being as distinctly developed as the sharp extended wings and pointed tail. The colour, moreover,—as in all these Tynet fossils—was ferruginous, instead

of being black, like the ichthyolites of Cromarty.
The specimen before me measured about four
inches and a half in length, and four inches and
a quarter from point to point of its wings—exclusive of the matrix.   These are supposed by Agassiz not to be organs of locomotion, but a defence
against its enemies, on the approach of whom it
suddenly extended them, as the perch erects its
dorsal fin, or a stickleback its spines, for a similar
purpose.   With the exception of the difference in
colour to which I have alluded, and a more perfect
head, the following brief quotation from Miller
will give you a familiar notion of the profile of the
pterichthys of Tynet burn.   "Imagine the figure
of a man rudely drawn in black on a grey ground :
the head cut off by the shoulders ; the arms
spread at full, as in the attitude of swimming ;
the body rather long than otherwise, and narrow-
ing from the chest downwards ; one of the legs
cut away at the hip-joint, and the other, as if to
preserve the balance, placed directly under the
centre of the figure, which it seems to support.
Such, at first glance, is the appearance of the
fossil."

There are portions of another fish, nearly allied
to the *pterichthys*, in this collection—the *coccosteus*, or berry-bone.   It was covered with an

armour of bony plates, closely dotted all over with berry-like protuberances—whence its name. On examining a drawing of the *coccosteus* restored to its original appearance, any one acquainted with the fish of the present day would class it with the rays. Miller compares it to a boy's kite. These two ichthyolites bear no resemblance to their contemporaries, which indeed, however they may vary from each other in form and dimensions, and in the character and position of their fins and scales—and therefore deserve the numerous generic and specific distinctions of Agassiz—yet even to an unscientific eye are as unmistakably *fish* as the carp or tench of modern waters. Unfortunately, there are no English names by which they can be recognized, but their classical titles—derived from the Greek—are singularly appropriate, and happily distinguish the more obvious peculiarities of each.

To speak broadly, they may be classed in two divisions, corresponding with Cuvier's great orders of *Malacopterygii* and *Acanthopterigii*—viz. soft-finned fishes, and thorny-finned fishes. The carp and tench are familiar modern examples of the first; the perch of the second. To begin with the former. The *glyptolepis*—carved or sculptured scale—must have been rather a short

I

and deep fish. It was covered with large circular
scales, so enormous when compared with the size
of the animal, that a specimen not more than half
a foot in length, has been known to exhibit scales
three-eighths of an inch in diameter, and in
another larger fragmentary example, whose entire
length would not have exceeded a foot and a half,
the scales were fully an inch across. These, when
examined with the microscope, reveal the most
delicate and intricate sculpturing.

The *Osteolepis*—or bony scale—is nearly allied.
The scales, though less, are yet large in proportion to the size of the animal. The position of
the fins is remarkable. The anterior portion of
the body seems to be destitute of them, but they
crowd together on approaching the tail. The
ventral fins are opposite to the space that occurs
between the two dorsals, and the caudal—or tail
—is unusually developed on the lower side.
These organs must have been marvellously constructed. In existing fishes, as Miller remarks,
"the membrane is the principal agent in propel-
ling the creature; it strikes against the water as
the membrane of a bat's wing strikes against the
air; but in the fin of the *Osteolepis*, as in those
of many of its contemporaries, we find the condition reversed. The rays were so numerous, and

lay so thickly side by side, like the feathers in the wing of a bird, that they presented to the water a continuous surface of bone, and the membrane only served to support and bind them together."

The *Cheirolepis*—literally, scaly hand, but as applied to a fish, signifying scaly pectoral fin—has a beautiful representative in this collection. The scales, unlike those in the two last-described fossils, are exceedingly small, and seem to run in minute wavy diagonal lines from the shoulder backwards, and the fins are similarly clothed. This specimen measures—exclusive of the matrix —fourteen inches and a half in length, and four in diameter.

Of the thorny-finned order—*Acanthopterygii*— perhaps the most common is the *Cheiracanthus*, or thorny hand. I have found several fore-shortened examples myself of this ichthyolite at Tynet burn, but its precise external form is seldom represented in the fossils, as it is generally more or less distorted; doubled up, as it were, with its tail almost in its mouth, as if it had expired in agony, and been petrified in that attitude.* Where this occurs, the nodule is

---

* I am since indebted to Mr. Simpson, of Tynet, for a remarkably fine specimen of The *Cheiracanthus*, from his own collection, representing the fish in perfect profile.

simply oval, without any prominences whatever to indicate the position of either extremity. The *Cheiracanthus* was covered with small enamelled scales, and possessed but one fin on the back, though several below. Their construction was remarkable; each seemed to consist of a single strong spine, to which a thin membrane was attached, so that in fact, as Miller says, "its fins are masts and sails, the spine representing the mast, and the membrane the sail."

In most examples of this little fish the head is very imperfect, doubtless from its having been composed principally of cartilage, but there is a good specimen here, only slightly foreshortened, in which the head is in an unusual state of preservation, the mouth being wide open, and the outline of both jaws distinctly portrayed.

Having now briefly described a few of the more striking of these ichthyolites, I will ask you to accompany me to the spot where, after the lapse of countless centuries, they were at length discovered, and exposed to the light of day. Were I more of a geologist or less of a sportsman, I might perhaps be ashamed to confess that, if the Spey had during that week been in a more propitious state for angling, the attractions of *Salmo salar* would have eclipsed those of *Cheirolepis* or

Pterichthys, but the water had for some time been provokingly low, and good sport could not be expected until after a change in the weather, which had latterly been exceedingly hot and sultry.

Tynet burn takes its rise in a wild elevated moorland district called White Ash hill, about three miles eastward of Gordon Castle, and flows for about five in a northerly direction parallel to the Spey, entering the sea about two miles to the east of that river. Except in the winter months, the quantity of water that finds its way through its channel would hardly entitle it to higher rank than that of an English brook, but the rapidity of its stream has enabled it, during countless centuries, to work its way through successive strata of conglomerate and sand-rocks of every quality and consistency. A walk of between two and three miles across the park and the great fir-woods—between the tall trunks of which I caught a glimpse of the bright water of Ortegarr—brought me to a bridge crossing the burn, below which, at no great distance from each other, are two small water-mills. Near the lower of these, the stream is overhung by a perpendicular section of a round hill, through which it has gradually eaten its way. It hardly deserves the name of a precipice, as the height can scarcely exceed thirty feet. Here, however, about twelve or fifteen feet from the base, are the remains ·of the fish-bed where the interesting collection of fossils were exhumed by Mr. Lennox, and many specimens in the unrivalled collection of the late Lady Gordon Cumming of Altyre, the rarity and perfection of which excited even the admiration of Agassiz.

I had been referred for any practical information I might require to an intelligent observer residing in the immediate neighbourhood,* whom I found most obliging and ready to impart it. He accompanied me to the spot, but held out no hope of a successful exploration on my part. In fact, he told me plainly, that "the golden age" was past, that the fish-bed was nearly exhausted, and that the prizes obtained a few years ago could not be equalled by the results of any future labours. He pointed out to me that the débris which had fallen from the upper surface of the cliff—the till, or glacial drift—had obscured, and

* Mr. Simpson, who, when this fish-bed was a virgin mine for explorers, made a valuable collection of these fossils, the greater part of which he subsequently presented to Sir Roderick Murchison, by whom they were deposited in the Museum of Practical Geology attached to the Geological Survey of Great Britain, in Jermyn Street, London; an institution whose good fortune it was, for many years, to possess as its chief "The Emperor of Siluria."

indeed choked up the residue of the fish-bed, and until this was removed even partial success was out of the question. A few seasons of heavy rain, hard frost, and subsequent thaws had loosened the consistency of the upper stratum of mould and gravel, portions of which were arrested in their descent, and patches of broom and gorse had consequently taken root half-way down, actually appearing to grow out of a hard bed of conglomerate, while each succeeding year added to the ruins. Great was my disappointment, though I derived some consolation from discovering, at the base of the cliff, several small nodules, and some of even larger dimensions in the bed of the stream, under water, for which I continued to wade perseveringly during the remainder of the afternoon, and carried home the greater portion of them in my fish-bag.

Before dark that evening I had explored their contents. Although by no means sanguine on the subject, I had ventured to expect better luck, but my hands were at last weary of wielding hammer and chisel when my labour was only rewarded occasionally by a mere ferruginous spot in the centre of the nodule, or a few scales or spines, or at best, by the tail or some fragment of an ichthyolite. By far the greater number contained nothing at all. Success was evidently out of the question until I could get at the fish-bed itself.

With the assistance of two able-bodied quarry-men, who worked hard for a couple of days, a considerable portion of the accumulated rubbish and several dangerous projecting masses over-head were finally removed, and this part of the cliff at length presented a different appearance. The base near the stream was composed of several layers of hard sandstone, perfectly distinct from each other, yet varying but little in colour or consistency; alternating with these were occa-sional seams of pudding-stone or conglomerate, all, less or more, of a ferruginous or deep-red tint, above which, about fifteen feet from the burn, a drab-coloured layer—apparently marl or indu-rated clay—had been exposed, studded here and there with nodules of the same appearance as those I had already found in the stream, but so firmly imbedded in the shale that it required the use of a small pickaxe, especially made for the purpose, to remove them without injury. This was the face of the fish-bed, or rather, all that remained of it, which I was enabled to reach by a narrow sloping terrace, or shelf, immediately underneath. The diameter of the marly stratum and the size of its nodules had diminished considerably since its first discovery, the centre of the bed, the tomb of the largest ichthyolites, having long since been despoiled of its treasures. Enough, however, remained to encourage a trial. Need I say with what energy I commenced operations, or how hopefully I continued to work until I had extracted nearly a hundred nodules, few of which, however, contained anything worth preserving. Gradually, my zeal was beginning to flag, when suddenly one of a form rather unusual, and of considerable size, attracted my attention, as it stuck half-way out of the marl. Instead of being oval, the portion that protruded was rather oblong, but the angles were unequal. In fact, when removed, it represented roughly, but correctly, the outline of a fish, the obtuse end of the sarcophagus enclosing the tail, the opposite extremity being rounded, while even the dorsal and ventral fins had their corresponding projections. With what breathless suspense did I apply the hammer! A vertical blow soon separated it into two parts, and the chisel gradually revealed to my delighted eyes, first the anterior half, then the remaining portion of a beautiful *Osteolepis*. The bones of the head, which are generally found to be dislocated, were nearly in their proper places, while the entire body was covered with scales like a coat of armour, and as brilliant as mother-of-pearl. In fact, although of moderate dimensions, it was fresher and more distinct than any specimen I had hitherto seen.

Several subsequent visits have I since paid to the same spot, and although I have frequently succeeded in securing small specimens of *Cheiracanthus*, *Cheirolepis*, and *Diplacanthus*, and even fragmentary plates of *Coccosteus* and *Pterichthys*, yet on none of these occasions have I felt such a thrilling interest as when I discovered my first perfect *Osteolepis* in the fish-bed of Tynet burn.*

* The fish-beds of Clune and Lethenbar lie about thirty miles to the westward, near the Findhorn river.   It is related by Mr. Duff, in his sketch of the Geology of Moray, that the nodules in that locality being composed of crystallized fibro-carbonate of lime, and therefore of the purest quality for cement or for agricultural purposes, were for several years burned into lime shells, and many were the valuable specimens of fossil fishes that were sacrificed in the operation.   It is told by the people in the neighbourhood that the late proprietor, suspecting that the nodules contained lime, sent specimens of them to Edinburgh to be analyzed, and received them back with the assurance that they were of pure lime and adapted for useful purposes ; but the included ichthyolites were not noticed, and the work of destruction went on till Dr. Malcolmson detected them and informed the scientific world of their great interest.

ALT DERG.

—◆—

" Quodque fuit campus, vallem decursus aquarum
Fecit ; et eluvie mons est deductus in æquor."

OVID.

ONE of the most remarkable spots amidst the peculiar scenery of the sandstone hills near. Gordon Castle is Alt Derg—or the red burn—although the latter title can convey no idea of its extraordinary configuration or peculiarities, for the bed of the so-called " burn " is now perfectly dry during summer and autumn, although it is doubtless to the long-continued erosive action of running water during past centuries, aided by the alternate influence of frost, rain, and melted ice and snow, that the deep excavation of the main glen is to be attributed, as well as of those tributary fissures that run in on either side, through which in bygone ages a cumbrous burden of rocks, mud, stones, and gravel was discharged into the bed of the Spey, and finally swept down by successive spates into the ocean itself.

I have already referred to the striking aspect of this gorge as it presents itself to a spectator from the opposite or left bank of the river, the previous course of its tributaries through the pine-covered hills being marked by zigzag lines of comparatively diminutive proportions, gradually increasing in depth and extent as they approach its termination, where, rising from its steep sides clothed with larch and firs, numerous tall, cylindrical cones of conglomerate shoot up from amidst the foliage of the trees, like gigantic sentinels keeping watch and ward over the entrance of the glen.

Alt Derg is about a couple of miles from Fochabers, from whence the road lies along the higher grounds on the right, looking down on the haughs and slopes above the Greenbank pool and the Cruive dyke, after which a path winds about for a little way among undulating ground, and it is not until you arrive at the very margin of the ravine that its immediate vicinity is indicated by any feature of the surrounding scenery. The bed beneath appears to be thickly strewed, as far as the eye can reach on either side, with smooth boulders and stones of every imaginable colour;

and looking down, as I did, for the first time, on
this variegated pavement during a sudden burst
of sunshine after a heavy shower of rain, the
whole scene was almost enough to enable me to
realize, for a moment, the fabulous but fascinat-
ing description of Sindbad's valley of precious
stones in "The Arabian Nights." A narrow
track, winding down along the steep side, leads
to the bottom, and on arriving there, the peculiar
character of the scenery becomes even more striking. It is impossible to resist the conviction that
you are walking over the dry bed of what must
have been at some former—and, geologically
speaking, not very distant—epoch, a powerful
torrent. All the loose stones under your feet are
rounded and water-worn, and although the sides
of the main glen are less precipitous than those
of the lesser fissures that run in diagonally, yet
the erosive action of the water can be traced where
the lower and more indurated portions present
occasionally sharp perpendicular sections, above
which the natural woods of spruce and larch seem
to cling with difficulty, and to sprout out in
almost impossible places, while every now and
then a ferruginous peak, like a great sugar-loaf, or
two in juxtaposition, like Siamese twins, shoot up
from the midst, in striking contrast to the sur-

rounding verdure. These eminences were doubtless originally cut by water out of a conglomerate
composed chiefly of materials from the under-
lying Silurian beds and forming part of the middle
division of the old red sandstone formation, and
would appear to owe their present configuration to
atmospheric influences. Successive frosts and
rains gradually decompose the softer material,
which is slowly washed away, and the same process, continued annually, leaves at last nothing but
the denuded and comparatively hard portion adhering to the central *backbone*, as it were, of these
elevated cones and turrets.

Following the eccentric course of the burn
towards the hills, and trudging laboriously through
the loose boulders under your feet, new scenes,
though of limited extent, are continually disclosed,
as each in succession vanishes from your view;
while, with the bright sunshine falling upon many
a little promontory of fantastic form projecting
into the foreground and lighting up the recesses
of the larch and fir-groves above—the opposite
banks being at the same time veiled in dark
shadow—you feel that, at every turn, an artist
would gladly linger, for the sake of adding a
charming vignette to the pages of his sketch-
book.

Some of the lesser ravines which run in on either side present a totally different appearance, although they must formerly have served as tributary watercourses to the main stream. One of these, near the mouth of the gorge, which I carefully explored, was not more than eight or ten feet wide, and became still more contracted as I clambered up its irregular ascent, over débris of large stones and sharp, angular blocks that lay in the very centre of its bed. The steep sides of this cleft could not have been less than thirty feet high, and the escarpment on either side was quite perpendicular, reminding me of one of those narrow streets of lofty houses, in certain old fortified German towns, that debouche at the bottom of a steep hill into the principal thoroughfare. The walls of the fissure to a great height exhibited a mass of conglomerate, but above this I perceived that the upper portion of the cliff was composed of the till, or glacial drift, overlaying the more ancient formation, of a somewhat lighter colour, but nearly resembling it in character and consistence. The depth of these beds varied remarkably. Immediately over my head the deposit was of unusual thickness, without any traces of stratification, and containing angular stones, rocks, and pebbles, indiscriminately scattered through the whole. One of considerable size at my feet appeared to have but recently fallen, a portion of the clay in which it was imbedded still adhering to it, and on looking up to discover the place from which it must have dropped, I perceived another of nearly equal dimensions projecting at right angles from the cliff, and suspended, like the sword of Damocles, over my head. So slight a hold did it appear to have in the loose boulder clay, that the report of a gun, discharged from the bottom of the narrow chasm where I stood, would probably have caused it to fall immediately. All the rocks in this part of Scotland are more or less covered by this deposit, composed of débris carried down from the distant mountains by the moving masses of land ice that annually swept over the country during the glacial epoch. At a subsequent period the gradual formation of water-courses followed. These, excavating their channels, slowly but surely, during countless centuries, have eaten their way alike through the superincumbent drift and the more indurated mass of conglomerate beneath. The professed geologist, indeed, can discover many other places in this district, and on the banks of the Spey itself, calculated to illustrate these interesting facts, but the lover of nature will not appreciate scientific truth the less from its being associated with such novel and quaint scenery as is exhibited in the gorge of Alt Derg and its tributary ravines.

BIRDS.

" The Eagles are gone ! "
Troilus and Cressida.

IN the heart of the great pine-woods that stretch
over the hills, north-east of the park, but below
the gorges that wind their way upwards through
the red sandstone slopes, lie two or three little lochs
much frequented by wild-ducks and other water-
fowl during the autumnal and winter months.   So
completely are they excluded from view by the surrounding forest that a stranger might fail to discover
their whereabouts, even after a prolonged search,
and the first intimation of his success would probably be the whirring sound of a party of ducks or
teal over his head, alarmed by the cracking of dead
sticks under his feet, or, if the weather happened
to be calm and bright, by the reflection of the
sunshine from the surface of the water piercing
through the tall stems of the fir-trees.

The most beautiful and least elevated of these secluded tarns is called Ortegarr—its old Gaelic title. The first time I visited it was during a stormy day, with three or four other gunners, for the express purpose of getting a shot at the wild-fowl, rough weather proving favourable for the sport, as they then quit the tempestuous estuary at the mouth of the river and the exposed lagoons along its sides, and seek the comparatively sheltered waters of this loch. The continuous roar, too, of the wind through the pine-trees is all in favour of sport, as the approach of the shooters stealthily crawling towards the margin, from opposite directions, is less likely to be revealed to the watchful birds by the snapping of dead branches or any other sound, and on this occasion each of us succeeded in reaching his own especial little screen of boughs, constructed near the banks, before any of them were alarmed. Presently a whirring of wings and a loud quacking, followed by two or three shots from the opposite side, told that we were discovered, and a brisk fusillade commenced. Mallards, ducks, and teal flew over our heads within easy distance, and many fell at the first volley. Then circling round several times in detached parties, they presented more difficult shots, but by our remaining in concealment, some of the

K

less timid descended again towards the water, either singly or in reduced numbers, and passing within fatal distance of a screen, would drop to rise no more, until by degrees even the last stragglers vanished and all was over for that day.

A year or two afterwards, during a long spell of sultry, cloudless weather in the early part of September, I was again wandering through these woods, with no companion but my spy-glass, in hopes of meeting with my old friends the cross-bills, *Loxia curvirostra*, or perhaps the still rarer crested titmouse, *Parus cristatus*, which I have never succeeded in detecting, although I knew that the species had been observed about thirty miles higher up the Spey, near Grantown, as well as still further south in the pass of Killiekrankie. After a fruitless search of some hours I found myself close to Ortegarr, and—on this occasion with the most friendly intentions towards the birds that frequented it—I commenced crawling through the heather in that direction as slowly and cautiously as possible. I was well rewarded for my trouble, and succeeded at last in reaching a slightly elevated mound, but a few yards from the edge, where, through a vista between the fir-trees that fringed the bank, I commanded a view of the greater part of the little sheet of water. It was a beautiful sight. Within twenty yards of me were a roebuck and a rae browsing leisurely on the succulent grasses near the margin. Farther on the left lay a little swampy island densely clothed with wild iris, bulrushes, and other aquatic plants of various colours, and on the intermediate water were several mallards, ducks, teal, coots, moor-hens, and little grebes swimming about and occasionally disappearing among the rank herbage or emerging from its recesses ; while knee-deep at the very edge stood a stately heron, motionless as a statue, intently watching for his prey. This part of the pool was slightly overshadowed by the reflection of the tall trees behind, but farther off the bright sun fell upon the water, lighting up at the same time the interior of the spruce firs and larch groves that clothed the more distant banks. In the very centre of the loch a cormorant was fishing by himself, incessantly diving and remaining a long time beneath, but rarely succeeding in capturing anything but very small eels. Every now and then a shadow, like a little cloud, would pass overhead, and a heron would sail through the still air or flap heavily along the surface of the water until he took up his position among the shallows in the distance. After watching this peaceful

K 2

scene for some time, I perceived that the roedeer
were becoming gradually aware of my presence,
having evidently "got my wind." First they
raised their heads and stared almost incredulously
at my place of concealment, as if doubting the
possibility of an enemy having approached so near
them without discovery. Then suddenly taking
alarm, they trotted off rapidly into the depth of the
forest. Next the heron rose from the extremity
of the little island where he had so long remained
motionless, and, extending his legs behind him,
flew lazily to the other end of the tarn, rousing
the cormorant on his way, who with a more rapid
flight quitted the scene altogether and disappeared
over the trees in the direction of the river. In
the meantime many of the wild-ducks and teal,
having taken wing immediately after the departure
of their friend and sentinel, the heron, collected
together in small parties and continued to circle
over my head, ever increasing their distance, but
apparently unwilling to quit their favourite haunts,
until at last, finding they had no just cause for
disquietude, they gradually approached the water
again, and finally settled down at the further extremity of the loch.

I rejoice to say that the herons are strictly pre-

L. Weld del.

M & N Hanhart lith.

ORTE GARR

served and their numbers consequently increasing. Their nests are not visible from the banks of the tarn, but I found several among the Scotch firs at a little distance. Would that the protection here afforded to these interesting birds were extended to them generally in the north, as well as to the larger and nobler members of the *Falconidæ*, which have now become exceedingly rare, and appear doomed to total extinction.

During my many visits to this part of Scotland, I never had the good fortune to see the golden or sea eagle on the wing, along the lower course of the Spey or in the deer-forests of Glenfiddich and Blackwater. It is true that there are no eyries of either species in this district, and it is in such situations—as the inland precipices of the Grampians, and the sea-cliffs of the northern and western coasts—that the principal destruction takes place. The excessive preservation of grouse and the value of the eggs of the golden eagle, *Aquila chrysaëtos*, to collectors, have principally tended to reduce the numbers of that magnificent bird, while the depredations of the sea eagle, *Haliæetus albicilla*, among young lambs, with which he occasionally varies his fish diet, have doomed him to persecution by the shepherds as well as gamekeepers; but in the eyes of the experienced forester the former species, at any rate, appears in a different light. He knows him to be a valuable ally to the deer-stalker as a check upon the inordinate increase of the prolific blue hare, *Lepus variabilis*, which indeed constitutes his favourite prey. Every stalker can call to mind how many a goodly stag has escaped from his rifle, just, perhaps, at the very moment when success seemed almost certain, through one of these animals suddenly starting up in front of him, running towards the nearest hinds and effectually alarming those watchful sentinels, before the desired range was obtained. During the autumn of 1862 I passed a week or ten days in the forest of Bræmar, in the heart of the Grampians, and besides good sport, deer-stalking, I had the additional pleasure almost every day of observing the golden eagle in his native haunts. I well remember my first view of the noble bird in this forest. He was soaring at a great height, every now and then arresting his career and hovering in the air like a kestrel, apparently watching some victim in the far heather below, and attended by a rabble rout of lesser birds, which, even allowing for distance, I could hardly believe to be larger than jackdaws. On examining them

through my spy-glass, I perceived that they were
hooded crows, who kept up their vain but pertina-
cious annoyance as long as he remained in view.
My surprise, however, was not greater than my
delight when the forester pointed out the royal
nest on an old Scotch fir-tree, which, with several
others, at some distance from each other, studded
the side of a hill near the base of Ben y Bourd.
Every ornithological authority that I was acquainted with had invariably assigned lofty inland
crags and precipices to the golden eagle as the
situation of his eyrie ; and, indeed, the high cliff
behind Corriemulzie, where he used to breed, owes
its present title to the circumstance, but this was
the only instance I had ever known of the nest
being constructed in a tree. Such is the result of
preservation ; or, in other words, the absence of
persecution, for the services of the eagle have
been long appreciated and the birds themselves
protected by the proprietor of the forest, so that
it would really appear as if the establishment of
confidence had rendered them less anxious to
select an inaccessible position for their eyrie. The
nest itself was not above twenty feet from the
ground, built on one of the larger horizontal
branches extending from the naked trunk ; and,

with the assistance of a gillie, I succeeded in climbing to it and examined its structure and contents. The enormous fabric was about eight feet wide. Some of the external sticks of which it was composed were nearly as thick as my wrist, their size gradually diminishing towards the centre, which was lined with birch twigs and heather. In the interior was an addled egg, where it had remained since the previous spring, white, like that of the sea eagle, and without any of the ferruginous or reddish colour that is more characteristic of the golden eagle's— although this pale variety is occasionally found even among prolific eggs of the latter species. Besides this, the nest contained several large wing and tail-feathers of the owner, a quantity of down —from the young birds—the foot of a blue hare, the wing and leg of a ptarmigan, and the half-devoured body of a recently killed hooded crow. It was evident that the parents still used it as a larder, which was satisfactorily explained, a few days afterwards, on my perceiving two immature golden eagles, whose ringed tails were distinctly visible through my spy-glass, flying about the tree and alighting occasionally on the ground, evidently expecting to be fed by their parents, neither of whom, however, appeared on that occasion, although repeatedly summoned by the loud screams of the younger birds.

For several years the golden eagle has established its eyrie on a Scotch fir in this forest. A stout bough, with strong lateral branches, is selected in the first instance, and the nest, such as I have described, constructed on the platform. In the following spring the fabric, even when apparently uninjured by the winter storms, is added to, or "put out" as the foresters call it. The same process is repeated annually, until at length the overburdened bough gives way and snaps off, carrying with it to the ground the accumulated mass of sticks, brushwood, and heather, and next year a new tree is chosen for the eyrie, sometimes at a great distance from that which had been previously occupied.

I may here mention, *en passant*, that while at Bræmar I had the first, and only opportunity during my life, of seeing the goshawk—*Astur palumbarius*—in a state of nature. A female of this species, in adult plumage, passed quite close to me, on two occasions, while returning in the evening from deer-stalking, near the top of Glenderry. The short wings, long tail, and transversely barred breast were of course conspicuous, and once I could even perceive the yellow iris. Altogether the bird was a gigantic representative of the sparrowhawk—*Accipiter nisus.*

In the neighbourhood of Gordon Castle, along the lower district of Spey, or in the deer-forests of Glenfiddich or Blackwater, I never observed either the golden or the sea eagle, but I have occasionally seen the osprey, *Pandion haliæetus,* circling overhead, and following the course of the river, although at a great height from the water. A bird of this species frequently takes up his quarters at Glenfiddich during the autumn, where I rejoice to say he is now safe from persecution, and where his depredations are exclusively confined to the small trout that abound in the mountain tributaries of the Spey. The Rev. Dr. Gordon, in his notes of the fauna of Moray, published some years ago in *The Zoologist,* says, that the osprey used to build in the ruins of Lochaneilan, Badenoch, and that a nest has also been found at Almore, in Glenmore. The species is, however, becoming rarer every day. Any one who has had the good fortune to witness its graceful flight and marvellous mode of fishing, will regret its approaching disappearance, as an indigenous bird, from the British fauna; and the same remark applies to the kite—miscalled *Milvus*

vulgaris. Truly this specific title must have been
applied to it in very different times from the present.
I have never seen one on the wing in this part of
Scotland. It has become in fact a *rarissima avis,*
even in those districts where it used to be abundant;
the result of constant persecution. I may, perhaps, be allowed here to quote from a former
little work of my own,* a list of " vermin "
destroyed on the Glengarry property, furnished to
me by a friend, who was himself the lessee of the
shootings at the time—from 1837 to 1840—and
by whose orders the slaughter was carried into
effect. If we remember that this system has been
carried out generally for many past years throughout Scotland, with a view to the preservation of
grouse, the excessive rarity of the larger species
of *Falconidæ* at the present day can no longer be
a matter of surprise. Numerous keepers were
employed in this wholesale massacre, who received
not only liberal wages, but extra rewards, varying
from £3 to £5, according to their success in the
work of extermination. The ornithologist will be
a little puzzled by the titles given to some of the
Raptores, but the names and epithets applied to
the greater number of them are, nevertheless,
unusually clear and appropriate, and will leave

* "Game Birds and Wild Fowl. Their Friends and their Foes."

no doubt in his mind as to the identity of some of the rarer victims. On this occasion I have omitted the quadrupeds, who figured equally in this black list :—

27 White-tailed Eagles.	462 Kestrels, or red hawks.
15 Golden eagles.	78 Merlin hawks.
18 Ospreys, or fishing eagles.	9 Ash-coloured hawks, or large blue-tailed ditto.
98 Blue hawks, or peregrine falcons.	83 Hen harriers, or ring-tailed hawks.
275 Kites, commonly called salmon-tailed gledes.	6 Jerfalcon, toe-feathered hawks (?).
5 Marsh harriers, or yellow-legged hawks.	1431 Hooded or carrion crows.
63 Goshawks.	475 Ravens.
7 Orange-legged falcons.	35 Horned owls.
11 Hobby hawks.	71 Common fern owls. *
285 Common buzzards.	3 Golden owls. †
371 Rough-legged buzzards.	8 Magpies.
3 Honey buzzards.	

But, since the ravages of the grouse disease, it may fairly be questioned whether the prevalence of that mysterious complaint may not be chiefly attributable to the removal of the natural checks on the inordinate increase of the species, fostered by so many contrivances, and notably by the destruction of those birds of prey whose favourite food they constituted. The weak and sickly, or superannuated members of a pack, were of course captured

---

* Probably the short-eared owl (*Otus brachyotos*). Surely not the insectivorous night-jar !

† The white or barn owl, comparatively rare in Scotland.

with facility, while the more vigorous and active escaped. Thus a sound stock survived for breeding, and the result was a healthy progeny, free from the admixture of a degenerate race of more numerous descendants, naturally liable to epidemic disease and premature decay. Every old grouse-shooter can call to mind how often in former times, when the peregrine was of comparatively common occurrence, he has experienced the vexation of seeing some of his wounded birds carried off by that powerful falcon, evidently selected as more easy victims than the rest of the pack. No predacious bird equals this species in courage and rapidity of flight. We may conclude, then, that sickly or otherwise debilitated grouse would generally fall to the share of the hen harrier, *Circus cyaneus*, formerly a common species, and still the least rare of the larger *Falconidæ*; of the marsh harrier, *Circus æruginosus*; of the common buzzard, *Buteo vulgaris*; and of the kite, *Milvus regalis*.

When fishing in the Spey near Boat o' brig, about five mile above Fochabers, I have frequently seen the peregrine falcon, *Falco peregrinus*. The great hill of Ben Aigen has two large fissures on the northern and north-western sides, which can be distinctly seen from here, in the steep escarp-

ments of which this falcon breeds, although the
nest is occasionally robbed of eggs or young.

Of indigenous owls, the long-eared—*Otus
vulgaris*—and the tawny—*Syrnium aluco*—are the
most common. The hootings of the latter may
still be heard every evening in the park, although
the species has certainly decreased in number
during the last few years. Indeed it is only
wonderful how it survives. On securing a rat or
young rabbit, the instinct of this owl—as well as
of many other rapacious birds—prompts it to fly
at once with its prey to a leafless stump or
pollarded tree, on the flat summit of which it
loves to feast uninterruptedly. Availing themselves of this habit, the wily keepers construct
the pole-trap—simply a board nailed horizontally
on the top of a post, ten or twelve feet from the
ground. No bait or lure is necessary: a naked
gin is placed on the flat piece of wood above: the
unfortunate owl flies unhesitatingly to the nearest
and is inevitably captured.

Among the numerous victims that adorn (?) a
conspicuous wall near the head keeper's residence,
the tawny owl seems to predominate. His com-
panions in disgrace, however, are sufficiently
numerous, principally kestrels, sparrow-hawks,
merlins, and a few hobbies, for the larger species

of *Falconidæ* have become so rare as seldom to find a place in this Golgotha.*

All the British members of the swallow family, *Hirundinidæ*, abound in the lower portion of Moray and Banffshire during the summer. The swift departs in July, but the rest remain far into the autumn. The chimney swallow and house martin are commonest. The sand martin, *Hirundo riparia*, is but partially distributed. The numerous cliffs and precipices along the banks of the Spey, and the sides of the dry watercourses and gorges intersecting the neighbouring hills, all in the red sandstone system, would appear at first sight to offer favourable situations for settlements of these birds during the breeding season, but such is not the case. I was much struck with a singular proof of this while examining the steep perpendicular side of a

* If these desultory remarks on some of the surviving *Falconidæ* should induce the ornithological reader to desire a more general acquaintance with the birds of this district—indigenous as well as migratory—he will find ample and trustworthy information on the subject in a work compiled from the journals and letters of the late lamented Charles St. John, and published since his decease, entitled "Natural History and Sport in Moray." A few very rare visitors have since been met with, such as Pallas's three-toed sand grouse, *Syrrhaptes paradoxus ;* the nutcracker, *Nucifraga caryocatactes ;* the roller, *Coracias garrula ;* and several examples of the greater spotted woodpecker, *Picus major ;* whose occurrence will be recorded at the end of this chapter.

quarry near the river. A few sand martins flying overhead induced me to believe that I should find some excavations of this species in the face of the prevalent strata. All these, however different in texture and composition—from the loose half solidified conglomerates and harder deposits, to the bands of fine friable sandstone and indurated layers of the same substance with which they alternated—were more or less coloured by red oxide of iron, and not one of them was pierced by the martin, but nearer the summit of the cliff a horizontal shallow belt of yellow sandstone— a comparatively recent formation—extended for several yards, exhibiting a single row of perforations nearly equidistant from each other, like the portholes of a gun-brig.

Of the many indigenous birds unjustly proscribed and gradually diminishing in number, the water ouzel, or dipper, *Cinclus aquaticus*, appears to me to be the most flagrant example, and I gladly avail myself of this opportunity of recording my belief that he is not only an injured innocent but an ill-used benefactor. For ages he has been condemned as a supposed devourer of trout and salmon spawn, but I am convinced that such a charge has no more foundation in truth than the once popular fables of cows and goats

being milked by the hedgehog and the nightjar.
I have had many opportunities of observing this
bird narrowly, more frequently in Ireland and
Wales than even in Scotland, and I may add—
though not without a slight pang of remorse—
that in the stomachs of the many specimens I
have shot and dissected, even when in the com-
mission of the supposed act of larceny, I never
could detect any portion of the spawn of either
trout or salmon. Let us for a moment watch the
manœuvres of a dipper. The scene shall be one
of his favourite haunts, the rocky banks of a
mountain burn, or the gravelly shallows of a
larger stream. Perhaps you are quietly seated
among the heather above, resting during the heat
of an autumnal noon, and admiring the various
colours of the mosses, lichens, and lycopodia that
clothe the margin. You are struck by the
loneliness of the scene. Nothing living appears to animate it. Suddenly a water ouzel
darts by, in swift, even flight, close to the surface,
and alights on a flat stone in the middle of the
burn a little lower down. You are no less struck
by his beauty—his snow-white breast contrasting
with his otherwise dark plumage—than with his
attitudes and performances: nodding his head
and jerking his short tail after the manner of a

wren, and then suddenly plunging into the stream, where you lose sight of him until he reappears on the surface in a few seconds a little lower down, and perhaps resumes his position on the same rock, or flies to a stone nearer the bank. You have probably read or heard that he can dive with facility and walk about at his ease on the gravelly bottom. Now is your time to watch his actions under water and to judge for yourself. You run quickly towards the spot, but are careful to check your speed and lie down before you reach it lest you should alarm him prematurely. Again he rises from the burn, rests for a moment on a stone, and soon disappears once more beneath the surface. Now you repeat your former manœuvre and reach the margin in time, above the very spot where he has just plunged into the clear shallow stream, and, looking down, you distinctly see him struggling with violent efforts to reach the bottom, towards which his head and neck are already protruded ; working his wings all the time with considerable exertion and *apparent* difficulty, quite unlike the comparatively facile movements of a coot or cormorant or any bird of similar specific gravity when in the act of diving. Now he seems to clutch the round pebbles for a few seconds and to be employed in extracting something from among them, but the ripple of the current prevents more accurate observation on your part. At last he comes once more to the surface, and, alarmed at your presence, darts along the burn. His flight is as even as that of a partridge, and he presents an easy shot. To satisfy yourself of his guilt or innocence, you—reluctantly—pull the trigger and he floats lifeless on the stream. Now for the trial. You carefully dissect his crop and stomach and examine their contents, and you discover several larvæ of *phryganeæ* and *ephemeræ*, minute beetles, and other aquatic insects, and several very small fresh-water snails,* but you search in vain for the ova of trout. Such an incident as I have just hurriedly described has occurred to myself repeatedly, and the result of my observations induces me to believe not only in the harmlessness of this interesting little bird—whose spring song, by the way, is exceedingly melodious, but that instead of being a destroyer of fish-spawn, he really assists in its preservation, by acting as a check on the increase of various predacious water-beetles, and other aquatic insects whose ravenous grubs or *larvæ* furnish his favourite food. His persecutors

* I have found sandhoppers, *Talitris locusta*, in the stomachs of some dippers killed on the banks of large rivers.

L

are therefore, in my humble opinion, amenable to
the double charge of injustice and ingratitude.

From the Moray Firth and the sheltered bays
of Dornoch and Cromarty on the opposite side,
vast numbers of wild-fowl pass over the Spey
during the latter part of the autumn on their way
to a more genial climate. About the end of October, if the weather happened to be severe, I have
seen herds of wild swans and flocks of geese and
marine ducks of various species flying overhead,
generally in a south-westerly direction, towards
Loch Ness. The temperature of this region,
however, although so far north, is comparatively
mild in early winter, heavy snow-storms seldom
taking place until January.

Some very rare visitors have occurred during
late years. The greater spotted woodpecker,
Picus major, had certainly been met with occasionally either singly or in pairs—as at Castle
Grant and near Inverness—but during the autumn
of 1868 the species appeared in unusual numbers
on both sides of the Moray Firth, showing that a
flock of " African woodpeckers "—as they were
there called—must have visited the north of Scotland. Mr. Yarrell notices that "although this bird
occurs in all the southern and midland counties
of England, it becomes rare on proceeding north-

wards. Nevertheless," he adds, " scarcely a year passes without some being obtained in Northumberland during October and November. This induces me to suppose that they are migratory in some of the more northern parts of Europe, perhaps in Norway and Sweden. They arrive about the same time as the woodcock and other equatorial migrants. . . . . . Mr. Selby says that he has seen it in Scotland on the banks of the river Spey, and amid the wild scenery of the Dee."* In Sussex, this bird is a spring arrival.

When visiting the Elgin Museum, in the same year, with the Rev. Dr. Gordon, he pointed out to me a honey buzzard which had been recently killed at Pluscarden, and a few days afterwards, being at Inverness, I had the opportunity of examining, *in the flesh*, at Mr. McLeay's, a beautiful specimen of the roller, *Coracias garrula*, which had been shot by a gamekeeper of the name of Nicholson, in the Oak Wood, and about ten days previously an example of the same rare visitor had been killed at Dornoch by Mr. Kerr Fraser. This species is said to have been met with in Orkney. It would appear to have a wide geographical range, and yet to be very partially distributed. It is very rare in England, of common

* YARRELL'S *British Birds.*

L 2

occurrence at Malta, during the spring and autumnal migration from Africa, scarce in France, unknown in Holland, but occasionally a wanderer to Sweden and Denmark.

That still more uncommon British visitor the nutcracker, *Nucifraga caryocatactes*, was killed about the same time at Invergarry. This species is a native of the pine forests of Russia and Norway, and is also found in Switzerland and among the Austrian Alps.

But the greatest ornithological curiosity that has ever been met with in this part of Scotland is the three-toed sand grouse, *Syrrhaptes paradoxus*, a specimen of which was shot by the Duke of Richmond, on the 23rd of October, 1863, out of a flock of seven or eight which he flushed while partridge-shooting on the banks of the Spey, between Gordon Castle and the mouth of the river. They rose from the shingle and at once attracted his attention by their rapid, swallow-like flight and unusual cry, and flew directly across the river.* This bird is a native of the steppes of Tartary, and until lately was unknown even as an accidental visitor to any part of Europe. The genus consists of a single species, and the

* Dr. Gordon informs me that a specimen was killed at Lossie-mouth, and another at Dornoch about the same time.

first instance of its occurrence in these islands was in July, 1859, when an individual shot by a labourer on Portreuddyn Farm, at the north end of Cardigan Bay, found its way to the Derby Museum at Liverpool.* In 1863, there occurred a regular irruption of these birds across Europe to the shores of England, and several specimens were obtained, principally in the eastern counties, since which period the migration has apparently ceased, and the sand grouse is once again a *rarissima avis*, more prized than ever by collectors, having now established its title to be considered a British bird. In an exhaustive article communicated to " The Ibis," Professor Alfred Newton has not only recorded the particulars of what he aptly terms " this Tartar invasion," illustrated by a sketch map, but given us an ample biography of the species, equally remarkable for scientific research and laborious investigation, as well as for the felicitous style which characterizes whatever falls from the pen of that distinguished ornithologist.

* Mr. T. J. Moore in " The Ibis," 1st series, Vol. II.

CAPTURE OF A LEVIATHAN.

—◆—

"Now hope exults the fisher's beating heart,
Now he turns pale and fears his dubious art:
He views the tumbling fish with longing eyes,
While the line stretches with th' unwieldy prize,
Each motion humours with his steady hands,
And one slight hair the mighty bulk commands."

GAY.

IT was the 14th of October, 1868, the last day
but one of the season. The sport during the
previous fortnight had been unusually good.
Frequent rains towards the close of September
had succeeded a long period of drought, and after
the clearing of the water many heavy fish—from
twenty-five to thirty-three pounds—had been
taken, while a few of still greater weight had
been observed "travelling" up stream. My
destination on that morning was to a part of the
river about five miles above bridge, comprising
three or four pools beyond Orton, and as the
evenings were now beginning to close in rapidly,

and I should have a long drive home, I started
immediately after breakfast, with the intention of
fishing down the river from the farthest point,
near Boat o' Brig, to the lowest pool allotted to
me for the day. I had killed four very heavy
salmon a few days before, near the sea, and hardly
expected now to surpass my previous good fortune, although perhaps entertaining a vague hope
that one of the aforesaid travelling monsters might
possibly have halted on his journey and taken up
his quarters in "the Garbity," or "the Couperee."
The weather was everything that could be desired
on the Spey. A light southerly breeze carried
the distant clouds across the sky, the air was
warm, but not oppressive, and the state of the
water, when I reached it, appeared equally propitious. It was lower than during the previous
week, but although perfectly clear, had that slight
coffee-coloured tint which is so favourable for
sport. On the left bank, just above where the
burn of Garbity falls in, there is a wooded island,
separated from the mainland by only a comparatively shallow arm, which is easily waded, but on
the other side, between it and Delfour, a deep and
exceedingly rapid stream rushes past, which in
very low water is generally considered a sure find
for a big fish, and although the river was just now

too full to give much hope of success at this spot,
I could not resist making the attempt; so putting
a "purple King" of medium size on a fine double
gut casting-line, I tried the entire reach, without
a rise or a pull; then changing my fly, but still
selecting one of the same size, I repeated the
process, wading this time so as to throw into the
deepest part of the channel, but was equally unsuccessful. I now adopted a gaudier lure—a
"Jock Scott"—but of similar dimensions to the
former, hesitating to use a smaller fly and lighter
tackle in so violent a stream, where, if taken by a
large fish, the struggle would probably end in his
escape; but the attractions of "Jock" were unavailing, and even a patient trial of a "silver
Doctor"—a regular syren in its way, that had
beguiled more than one salmon to its doom—was
equally unsuccessful. Below this was Garbity
pool, where, two years before, I had capital sport,
but on reaching its banks I was not a little disappointed to find its character completely changed.
The floods of previous winters had half-filled the
bed of the stream with gravel and boulders, and,
though of considerable extent, the entire sheet of
water was so dull and sluggish that it was impossible to work a fly well in any part of it. Just
at the tail, however, the current seemed to concen-

trate between several rocks and to increase in
force until, as a strong boisterous rapid, it joined
the head of the Couperee, one of the most extensive pools on this part of the river.   In full water,
when just clearing after a spate, heavy fish frequently lie within reach of the left bank, avoiding
the more turbulent stream in the middle, and the
best part can be commanded from the shore, but
in its present state they would more probably
frequent the central current, during the upper
portion of its course, and it was necessary to wade
through a labyrinth of submerged rocks, among
which it was no easy matter to advance and preserve at the same time a firm footing.   Once indeed
I was quite immersed, while feeling my way among
the conical slippery stones at the bottom.   Commencing, as usual, with as large and dull-coloured
a fly as seemed suited to the state of the water,
and changing it occasionally from the stock wound
round my fishing-hat, without going on shore, I
descended gradually from the upper part of the
pool until its increasing depth forbade a further
progress in that direction.   Here the main current wheeled nearer to the bank, from whence it
appeared quite possible to reach it with a long line
for a considerable part of its downward course,
and, feeling rather chilly from my previous duck-

ing, I was preparing to land, but yielded to the
temptation of taking one more cast before doing
so.   Throwing again therefore across stream, I
anxiously watched the fly as it swept round for
the last time, but just as I was on the point of
drawing it out, a sudden plunge a few inches
below it, followed by the apparition of a huge
dorsal fin above the surface, told that I had roused
the attention of a monster, although he had not
yet "tasted steel."   To stimulate his appetite
therefore by delay I pitched my fly several times
higher up, preserving carefully the same length of
line, and at last brought it again over him.   Every
salmon-fisher has experienced the excitement of
such a moment, and can sympathize with my feelings after thrice repeating the process in vain.
Even a change of fly proved ineffectual, until at
last, vexed, shivering, and disappointed, I waded
to the shore and sat down sulkily on the bank.
Just at that moment the clouds, which had hitherto floated in succession across the sky, disappeared
one by one, and for half an hour I basked luxu-
riously in the warm sunshine, smoked the calumet
of peace, and under its soothing influence admired the scenery in the neighbourhood of this
beautiful pool.

To the south, about a couple of miles off, rose

the lofty hill of Ben Aigen, rent with two deep clefts, their precipitous sides varied with grey primæval rocks, among which the peregrine falcon still rears its young in spite of constant persecution, while the farther cliff of the more distant corrie is covered to the very summit of the mountain with dark firs, and the nearer slopes are varied with purple heather and evergreen woods, with fissures of sandrock peeping through them, altogether presenting a charming contrast of colours in this part of the landscape. Immediately opposite were the lesser hills near Delfour, clothed with larch, spruce, and beech, and only separated by a wide-spreading bed of shingle from the river, which, after passing through Couperee, turned to the left on its way to Orton, and still farther north the red cliffs overhanging its waters near the Chapel pool stood out in bold relief from the gloomy pine forest behind them.

I had but little time, however, to spare for admiration even of this picturesque scene. The back fin of the big fish was still fresh in my memory and uppermost in my thoughts, and I did not yet despair of becoming more intimately acquainted with him. I perceived that the water had fallen considerably since the morning, and had become clearer and more transparent, suggesting

the use of single gut and a, much smaller fly than
any I had previously used.   Carefully turning
over every leaf of my book, I had half decided
more than once in selecting one, but as often
hesitated when I looked at the diminutive barb
and thought of the giant in whose jaws I fondly
hoped to fix it.   Suddenly I recollected that
among the larger flies, wound round the cork
band encircling my hat, was a very small one,
tied but a few days previously for me by that in-
comparable artist, Shanks, of Craigellachie, on a
minute double hook, a few of which I had procured on my way through London for the express
purpose of employing them in clear low water
with heavy fish.   The little beauty was a modest
Spey lassie, known as a " silver green," and not
larger than one of the lake trout-flies I had often
used in the west of Ireland.   The casting-line
and terminal loop were of single gut, by no means
thick, but perfectly smooth and cylindrical, every
link of which I had previously tested, selecting
only a few of the best from each hank.   Now for
the trial.   I had marked the spot where the fish
rose by placing a few stones on the top of the
bank immediately opposite, and perceiving that I
could reach it without difficulty from the shore,
I commenced a little higher up, increasing my

length of line as I advanced, and almost prophetically feeling, as I neared it, that the long rest I had given the pool, assisted by the change of fly and tackle, would rouse him to activity. Yes! he has it this time. A violent chuck under water that would infallibly have broken any but the very best gut, and whish—sh—sh, away he went like a runaway horse, carrying off sixty yards of line in a few seconds, towards the far side of the river. A momentary pause followed, but before I could avail myself of it, another rush succeeded in the same direction, and with dismay I saw that my reel was nearly empty and that my fish was already not far from the spot where a friend— another piscator, who had just arrived—stood up to his waist in the water at the opposite side of the pool, awaiting the issue of the combat before commencing operations himself. Away went the salmon again up-stream at a tremendous pace, trying to drown the hissing line as it cut its way through the opposing current, and I had to hurry along the bank to outflank him, expecting every moment before I could accomplish that manœuvre the usual spring into the air, and that the somersault, delivered backwards, would break it—a very probable contingency under the circumstances. But no; he still continued his rapid course under water, now, however, rather in an oblique direction, and as I had by this time got well above him, I was able to wind up quickly, preserving, at the same time, an equal and steady pressure, but, with due regard to the delicacy of my tackle, neither " showing him the butt," nor allowing the rod itself to descend from the perpendicular. Then followed a succession of tremendous rushes, first across, then up, and finally down stream, which last I encouraged by running with him along the bank and leading him, as it were, by gentle force, in the same direction. In this way we traversed nearly the entire length of the pool, but, contrary to my expectation, he showed no sign of exhaustion or change of tactics, and not having yet obtained even a glimpse of him to enable me to guess his weight, I began to think that I had *foul*-hooked a very heavy fish, that his capture would, under any circumstances, be a work of considerable time, and that if he should continue his present downward course a little longer, and get into the tail of the Couperee, and through a swift and turbulent reach into the Laird's pool, beset with sunken trees and snags, the chances were all against success. Fortunately, however, just as these forebodings were on the point of being realized, down he went to the very bottom and stopped. Not a moment was now to be lost. Five minutes' rest would restore all his previous power and activity, but a succession of boulders discharged rapidly and with unerring aim by the hand of Simon, and falling within a foot or two of his position, failed to rouse him from his sulky fit. So winding up quickly and advancing at the same time into the water, rather below my fish, where I found a sound, gravelly bottom, I was enabled to wade within a few yards of the spot, and, with a short line, attempted to lift him, as it were, towards the surface. In the event of a salmon being foul-hooked this manœuvre is generally fruitless, but if the fly is fixed within the jaws it is seldom a failure, and, to my delight, its effect on the present occasion was instantaneous. Off he went again towards the other side of the river, and then once more faced the stream. Now hurrying out of the water as quickly as possible, and scrambling up the bank, I got well above him, and at last I could feel that his strength was beginning to fail, as, notwithstanding the weight, I was able to increase the pressure of the rod without opposition, until I had wound up about forty yards of line spun out during his last run. Now he moved again submissively down stream, but suddenly, when I least expected it, made one final desperate effort, and rushed right over to a shallow at the other side of the pool where he had not been before, but quickly yielding to the rod, his back fin and the upper part of his tail appeared above the surface, showing, though but for a few seconds, his enormous proportions, before he rolled heavily into the deep water, as I gradually but steadily drew him towards the shore. Just at this moment I felt almost sure of success, as he was now comparatively reduced to obedience, when an unexpected crisis suddenly arrived.

A little below the fish, but nearer to me, I caught a glimpse of a small stump—a fragment of a submerged tree—projecting above the surface. In a few seconds all would be over unless I could force him to this side before the stream carried the line across it. Then, indeed, I ventured—in Irish parlance—to "show him the butt," winding-up and walking backwards at the same instant, with my heart in my mouth during that trying moment. It was "touch and go." The slightest effort on the part of the descending giant would have ensured his immediate escape, but how can I describe my delight as he passed between me and the terrible stump, although but a few inches from the latter. The rest may be briefly told. The

double hook, though of Lilliputian proportions
and severely tested, had proved faithful, and I felt
sufficient confidence in the nature and tenacity of
its hold to warrant me in bringing matters to a
speedy conclusion. A few more ineffectual efforts
to return to the stream, and again I led my captive
to the water's edge, where Simon was already
cowering under the bank, clip in hand, watching,
like a tiger in his lair, for the supreme moment.
It came at last. A splash, a plunge, and a fierce
struggle succeeded, and throwing down the rod, I
assisted him in landing an enormous salmon, in
beautiful order and of perfect proportions. Both
barbs of the " silver green " were fixed inside the
mouth, one of them securely, while the other had
been considerably bent backwards, and had nearly
lost its hold. Weight, forty-three pounds; length,
forty-six inches; girth, twenty-six; and, although
believed to be the heaviest that had ever been
taken by the rod on Spey, up to that time, yet, in
spite of my exultation, I could not but feel, as the
tug of war had been confined to a single pool, and
the enemy had never shown his colours during the
battle, that the incidents of the contest were of a
less exciting character than I had often experienced
with many a livelier fish of lesser weight and
inferior condition.

M

A WISH.

OH, tell me, kind angels, why is it,
　　When hundreds of miles far away,
That often in dreams I revisit
　　The banks of the glorious Spey ?

King David once ruled on the Jordan,
　　On the Tiber bold Cæsar had sway,
But Cæsar was "nocht" * to the Gordon,
　　And the Tiber a joke to the Spey.

And the Amazon, Nile, and Euphrates,
　　Are all very well in their way,
And the Shannon in land of "pitatees,"
　　But none can compare with the Spey.

Such fishing ! By Jupiter Ammon,
　　There's nothing like fishing, I say,
And especially fishing for salmon
　　In the pools of the galloping Spey.

Six weeks from the First of September
　　Ever pass like one beautiful day,
'Tis a time I shall ever remember,
　　A paradise pass'd on the Spey.

If I've any particular wish
　　Since my hair has grown grizzled and grey,
Why it is to be able to fish
　　Every year till I die, in the Spey.

---

* Nocht—nihil. JAMIESON'S *Dictionary of the Scottish Language.*

And when the grim tyrant draws near,
  And life s breath is ebbing away,
May all that is left of me here
  Repose on the banks of the Spey!

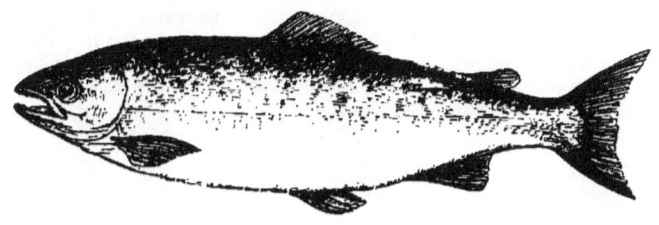

IN SPE VIVO

Woodfall and Kinder, Printers, Milford Lane, Strand, London, W.C

BOOKS ON BIRDS, ETC.

PUBLISHED, OR IN PREPARATION, BY MR. VAN VOORST.

HINTS ON SHORE SHOOTING, including a chapter on Skinning and Preserving Birds. By J. E. Harting, F.L S., F.Z.S. Post 8vo. 3s. 6d.

A HANDBOOK OF BRITISH BIRDS, 8vo. Showing the Distribution of the Resident and Migratory Birds in the British Islands, with an Index to the records of the rarer species. By J. E. Harting, F.L.S., &c.

THE ORNITHOLOGY OF SHAKESPEARE, Critically Examined, Explained, and Illustrated. By James Edmund Harting, F.L.S., F.Z.S. 8vo. 12s. 6d.

THE BIRDS OF MIDDLESEX. A contribution to the Natural History of the County. By James Edmund Harting, F.L.S., F.Z.S. Post 8vo, 7s. 6d.

YARRELL'S BRITISH BIRDS. Revised by Alfred Newton, M.A., Professor of Zoology and Comparative Anatomy in the University of Cambridge, &c., &c. In Parts at 2s. 6d. each.

FALCONRY IN THE BRITISH ISLES. By Messrs. Salvin and Brodrick. Second Edition, with new Plates and Additions. Imperial 8vo.

FALCONER'S FAVOURITES. By W. Brodrick, one of the Authors of "Falconry in the British Islands." A series of Life-sized Coloured Portraits of all the British species of Falcons at present used in Falconry. Large folio, cloth, £2 2s.

FALCONRY IN THE VALLEY OF THE INDUS. By R. F. Burton. Post 8vo, with Four Illustrations, 6s.

THE BIRDS OF THE HUMBER DISTRICT. By John Cordeaux, of Great Cotes, Ulceby. Post 8vo.

THE BIRDS OF NORFOLK. By Henry Stevenson, F.L.S. Vols. 1 and 2, 8vo, each 10s. 6d.; Vol. 3 will complete the Work.

THE BIRDS OF SOMERSETSHIRE. By Cecil Smith, of Lydeard House, near Taunton. Post 8vo, 665 pp., 7s. 6d.

THE BIRDS OF EGYPT. By G. Ernest Shelley, F.Z.S., F.R.G.S., &c., late Captain Grenadier Guards. Royal 8vo, with fourteen coloured Plates, price £1 11s. 6d.

NOTES ON THE BIRDS OF DAMARA LAND, AND THE ADJACENT COUNTRIES OF SOUTH-WEST AFRICA. By the late Charles John Andersson, Author of "Lake Ngami," and of the "Okavango River." Arranged and edited by John Henry Gurney, with some additional Notes by the Editor. 8vo.

BIRDS OF JAMAICA. By P. H. GOSSE, F.R.S. Post 8vo, 10s.

COLOURED ILLUSTRATIONS OF THE EGGS OF BRITISH BIRDS, with Descriptions of their Nests and Nidification. By WILLIAM C. HEWITSON. Third Edition, 2 vols. 8vo, £4 14s. 6d.

SYSTEMATIC CATALOGUE OF THE EGGS OF BRITISH BIRDS, arranged with a view to supersede the use of Labels for Eggs. By the Rev. S. C. MALAN, M.A., M.A.S. On writing-paper, 8vo, 8s. 6d.

BIRD LIFE. By DR. E. A. BREHM. Translated from the German by H. M. Labouchere, F.Z.S., and W. Jesse, C.M.Z.S., Zoologist to the Abyssinian Expedition. Parts, royal 8vo, 2s. 6d. each.

A NATURAL HISTORY OF CAGE BIRDS. By J. G. KEULEMANS, late Assistant to the Museum of Natural History of Leyden. Imperial 8vo. In parts, each containing Six Coloured Plates, 5s. each.

A DESCRIPTIVE CATALOGUE of the Raptorial Birds in the Norfolk and Norwich Museum. By JOHN HENRY GURNEY. Part I., royal 8vo, 5s.

MONTAGU'S DICTIONARY OF BRITISH BIRDS, containing a full account of the Plumage, Weight, Habits, Food, Migrations, Nest and Eggs of every Bird found in Great Britain and Ireland. Edited by EDWARD NEWMAN, F.L.S., F.Z.S., &c. 8vo, price 12s.

ORNITHOLOGICAL RAMBLES IN SUSSEX, with a Catalogue of the Birds of that County, and Remarks on their Local Distribution. By A. E. KNOX, M.A., F.L.S., F.Z.S. Third Edition, 7s. 6d.

AUTUMNS ON THE SPEY. By A. E. KNOX, M.A., F.L.S. Post 8vo, with Four Illustrations by Wolf.

THE IBIS: A Quarterly Journal of Ornithology. Edited by OSBERT SALVIN, M.A., F.L.S., F.Z.S., &c. 6s. each.

A HISTORY OF BRITISH FISHES. By WILLIAM YARRELL, F.L.S., V.P.Z.S. Third Edition. Edited by Sir John Richardson, C.B., F.R.S., &c. &c. 2 vols., 8vo, £3 3s.

This book ought to be largely circulated, not only on account of its scientific merits—though these, as we have in part shown, are great and signal,—but because it is popularly written throughout, and therefore likely to excite general attention to a subject which ought to be held as one of primary importance. Every one is interested about fishes—the political economist, the epicure, the merchant, the man of science, the angler, the poor, the rich. We hail the appearance of this book as the dawn of a new era in the natural history of England."—*Quarterly Review*, No. 116.

YARRELL.—GROWTH OF THE SALMON IN FRESH WATER. With Six Coloured Illustrations of the Fish of the natural size, exhibiting its structure and exact appearance at various stages during the first two years. 12s. sewed.

JOHN VAN VOORST, 1, PATERNOSTER ROW.

www.ingramcontent.com/pod-product-compliance
Lightning Source LLC
Chambersburg PA
CBHW022354020726
47500CB00002B/267